T0304467

MURDLE

THE SCHOOL OF MYSTERY

ALSO BY G. T. KARBER

Murdle: Volume 1

Murdle: Volume 2

Murdle: Volume 3

MURDLE

THE SCHOOL OF MYSTERY

50 SERIOUSLY SINISTER LOGIC PUZZLES

G. T. KARBER

ST. MARTIN'S
GRIFFIN
NEW YORK

First published in the United States by St. Martin's Griffin, an imprint of
St. Martin's Publishing Group

www.stmartins.com

Designed by Omar Chapa

Exhibits designed by Dani Messerschmidt

The Library of Congress Cataloging-in-Publication Data is available upon request.

ISBN 978-1-250-35071-8 (trade paperback)

Our books may be purchased in bulk for promotional, educational, or
business use. Please contact your local bookseller or the Macmillan
Corporate and Premium Sales Department at 1-800-221-7945, extension 5442,
or by email at MacmillanSpecialMarkets@macmillan.com.

First Edition: 2024

10 9 8 7 6 5 4 3 2 1

CONTENTS

EARNING YOUR DEGREE

When you complete a mystery correctly, give yourself a star in the box at the bottom of the grid. Additionally, there will be opportunities for extra credit in each section. When you've finished your tenure at Deduction College, head to Commencement on page 227 to earn your degree.

Will you graduate with honors . . . or with your life?

MURDLE

THE SCHOOL OF MYSTERY

HOW TO SOLVE

Welcome to *Murdle: The School of Mystery,* a curious collection of the college case files of the world's greatest mystery-solving mind, Deductive Logico.

Unlike other histories of the crime-solving life, these murdles are not mere tales, but puzzles for you to solve. And all you need to crack these cases is a sharp pencil and an even sharper mind.

To prove it, let's revisit one of Deductive Logico's more recent cases.

It had taken place in a big, mysterious bookstore, and as he stood there amongst the stacks, he knew that one of three people had committed the crime:

DAME OBSIDIAN

A mystery writer whose books have sold more copies than Shakespeare and the Bible put together.

5'4" • LEFT-HANDED • GREEN EYES • BLACK HAIR

CHAIRMAN CHALK

He figured out the publishing business years ago and never looked back. Yes, he called ebooks a "fad" and he still owns a rotary phone. He is worth a billion dollars.

5'9" • RIGHT-HANDED • BLUE EYES • WHITE HAIR

EDITOR IVORY

The greatest romance editor of all time. She invented the enemies-to-lovers genre, and she was the first person to put a naked man on the cover of a book.

5'6" • LEFT-HANDED • BROWN EYES • GRAY HAIR

Logico also knew that each of the suspects was in one of these places and had one of these weapons:

THE PUZZLE SECTION

Where they usually put the puzzle books. But *Murdle* could be anywhere, couldn't it?

THE MYSTERY SECTION

They have all the best Dame Obsidian whodunits, as well as all the worst Dame Obsidian whodunits.

THE SECRET BACK ROOM

Here is where they keep the special secret books they don't want you to buy.

A FOUNTAIN PEN
LIGHT-WEIGHT

The pen is mightier than the sword. Especially if you're using it to stab someone!

FIRE EXTINGUISHER
HEAVY-WEIGHT

Ironic that something intended to keep you safe could kill you. Or maybe just unfortunate.

A COPY OF *MURDLE: THE SCHOOL OF MYSTERY*
MEDIUM-WEIGHT

This very book could be used as a weapon. What a responsibility.

Now, Logico knew he could not make assumptions just from reading these descriptions. Sometimes mystery writers were in the puzzle section, and sometimes romance editors were reading murder-mystery puzzle books. No, the only way to figure out who had what where was by studying the clues and evidence.

These were the facts he knew to be absolutely true:

- Chairman Chalk was in the puzzle section.

- The person with the fountain pen was envious of the person in the back room.

- Dame Obsidian was carrying a medium-weight weapon.

- The tallest suspect had a seemingly ironic weapon.

- **The body was found in the secret back room.**

Logico pulled out his detective notebook and drew a grid, labeling each column and row with a picture representing each of the suspects, weapons, and locations.

The locations were listed twice—once on top, and once on the side—so that there was a square for every potential pairing. This tool—the deduction grid—was a powerful technology he had learned at Deduction College (Fig. 1).

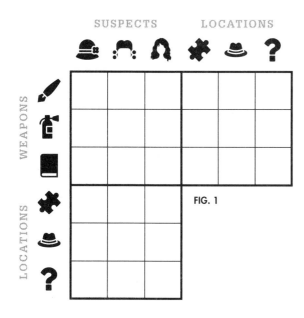

FIG. 1

But Logico was the first to use it to solve a murder, and boy, had he solved a lot of murders in college! Probably a statistically significant number. But he couldn't daydream about his college years now; he had to solve a mystery.

To do that, he would have to record on his grid the information he learned from each clue, starting with the first one:

Chairman Chalk was in the puzzle section.

That seemed straightforward enough, so Logico marked it down with a checkmark (Fig. 2).

But that was not all Logico learned from that clue. If Chairman Chalk was in the puzzle section, then he couldn't be in the mystery section or the secret back room. And since only one suspect was at each location, neither Dame Obsidian nor Editor Ivory were in the puzzle section with him. Logico represented those deductions on his grid with Xs (Fig. 3).

This illustrates a principle: when you identify somebody's location or their weapon, you can cross out every other possibility in that row and column.

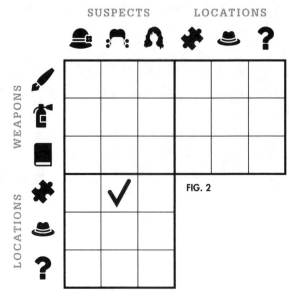

FIG. 2

SUSPECTS   LOCATIONS

WEAPONS

LOCATIONS

FIG. 3

Logico moved on to the next clue:

The person with the fountain pen was envious of the person in the back room.

It seems like this clue is telling you about personal relationships. But Logico was only concerned with facts. And the only fact this clue told him was that the person with the pen and the person in the back room were two separate people. Therefore, the pen was not in the back room.

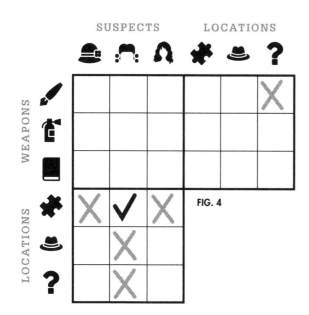

FIG. 4

And so, Logico marked that down on his deduction grid, too (Fig. 4).

He couldn't conclude anything else from there, so he moved on to the next clue:

Dame Obsidian was carrying a medium-weight weapon.

Logico looked through his notes and saw that the only medium-weight weapon was the copy of *Murdle: The School of Mystery*.

That must have been what Dame Obsidian was carrying.

Again, Logico could cross out an entire row and column! After all, if Dame Obsidian had a copy of this book, then neither Chairman Chalk nor Editor Ivory had it, and since each suspect

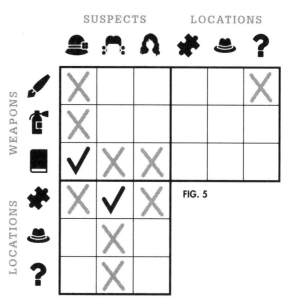

FIG. 5

can only have one weapon, Dame Obsidian couldn't have had the pen or the fire extinguisher, either (Fig. 5).

However, there is something else he can deduce here as well, and this is the key to all the puzzles in this book: if Chairman Chalk was in the puzzle section, and he didn't have a copy of *Murdle: The School of Mystery,*

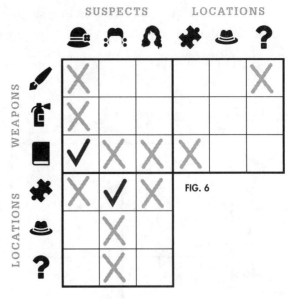

FIG. 6

then the book could not have been in the puzzle section, either (Fig. 6).

At first, this was confusing for Logico, but he had done it so many times it was easy for him now, and it'll be easy for you, too.

Then, Logico moved on to the next clue:

The tallest suspect had a seemingly ironic weapon.

In order to solve this one, Logico had to re-read the descriptions of each suspect to discover that Chairman Chalk was the tallest. Then, he had to re-read the descriptions of all the weapons to remember that one of them, the fire extinguisher, is described as being ironic.

That must mean that Chairman Chalk had the fire extinguisher.

You don't need to make leaps of logic in these puzzles: everything you need to know clearly appears in the descriptions.

Logico marked down that Chairman Chalk had the fire extinguisher, and he crossed off the other possibilities in that row and column. Once he did that, Logico was satisfied. If Dame Obsidian had the copy of *Murdle: The School of Mystery* and Chairman Chalk had the fire extinguisher, then he knew Editor Ivory must have had the fountain pen.

He marked all that down on his grid (Fig. 7).

But Logico could deduce even more from that clue: since Chairman Chalk had the fire extinguisher, and Chairman Chalk was in the puzzle section, then the fire extinguisher was in the puzzle section.

That means that the fountain pen had to have been in the mystery section, and *Murdle: The School of Mystery* had to have been in the secret back room (Fig. 8).

Therefore, because Editor Ivory had the fountain pen, which was in the mystery section, that's where Editor Ivory was too. And Dame Obsidian must have been in the secret back room.

The deduction grid

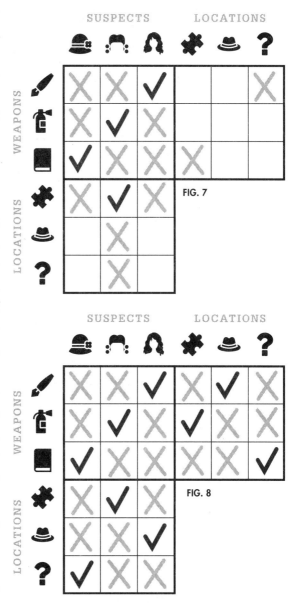

FIG. 7

FIG. 8

was complete! So satisfying, thought Logico. But he still didn't know whodunit.

So he was ready for the final, bolded clue:

The body was found by the books they don't want you to buy.

This last clue is special. It doesn't tell you who has what weapon where—it tells you about the murder itself!

By consulting his notes, Logico knew that this clue meant that the murder had been committed in the secret back room, because the description of the secret back room clearly says it's where they—whoever *they* is—keep the books they don't want you to buy.

Therefore, since according to Logico's grid Dame Obsidian was in the secret back room, and that's where the body was found, then Dame Obsidian must have committed the crime.

Confident in his deductions, as he always was, Logico gathered the suspects at the crime scene, where he walked them through the logic above, and then, finally, he made his accusation:

"It was Dame Obsidian with *Murdle: The School of Mystery* in the secret back room!"

Chairman Chalk was impressed with the savvy work, and offered Logico another book deal. Dame Obsidian, however, went on to write a bestselling book about it, entitled *Throw the Book at Me: An Idunit,* continuing her popular series of mysteries starring the famous author Lady Blackstone, who absolutely wasn't based on a thinly veiled version of herself.

But that would all come later.

At the time, Logico was staring at the cover of *The School of Mystery,* deep in thought. It carried him, through his memories, back to his time in Deduction College, and the things he'd learned, and the people he'd met, and, perhaps most important of all, the murders he'd solved.

This book contains fifty mysteries that Deductive Logico solved in Deduction College, using these techniques and many others. There are ciphers to decode, witness statements to examine, and many other secrets to unlock.

As you progress, and the mysteries become more challenging, you will find your reasoning skills put to the test. There will always be new techniques to learn and new deductions to master.

If you get stuck, do not despair! You can flip to the back of the book for a hint. And when you're ready to make your accusation, flip even farther back to the solutions to see if you're right. With every mystery you solve, a bigger mystery will emerge.

If you need more help, or want to solve more mysteries, then join the Detective Club at Murdle.com. Otherwise, you're on your own. Good luck, gumshoe!

FRESHMAN

Wisdom begins in wonder.

—Socrates, from Plato's *Theaetetus*

Freshman Logico was thrilled to attend Deduction College.

As he strolled across campus for the first time, he stared up at the beautiful brick towers of Old Main. He smelled the grass of the campus quad, where a speaker was addressing a circle of students. Others drank coffee in the campus coffeeshop, which doubled as the bookstore. A troupe of theater kids were already rehearsing an extracurricular play at the Greek Theatre.

He was excited to study the school's famous trivium—logic, grammar, and rhetoric—which they believed built the foundation of a well-reasoning mind, and its four primary subjects, the quadrivium—arithmetic, geometry, astronomy, and music.

Deduction College was incredibly prestigious, and Logico felt honored to be here. He was excited to learn as much as he could. For as long as Logico could remember, he had loved to study, to learn new facts, and to apply them in clever ways.

But Logico could not have predicted all that would happen to him in the four years he would attend Deduction College. He would be challenged in ways he had never expected, and be forced to make difficult decisions that would change his life forever.

One of the first things he learned, whispered to him by another student at orientation, was that the school's reputation was not as squeaky-clean as he had thought.

The first chancellor and the founder of the school, Lord Graystone, had been killed under mysterious circumstances at the founding of the school. And there were rumors of secret societies, hidden tunnels, political intrigue, and many, many mysteries to solve.

The following ten mysteries cover Freshman Logico's first year at school. In it, he would make alliances, encounter mysterious figures, and betray someone who trusted him.

If you find freshman year too easy, then there is an additional challenge for you. For extra credit, see if you can solve this riddle: each of the murders in this section was committed by a single person, but a shadowy figure was orchestrating them all, making sure the right people were killed by the right people in the right way.

Can you determine who is behind the murders before Logico?

A MAP OF DEDUCTION COLLEGE

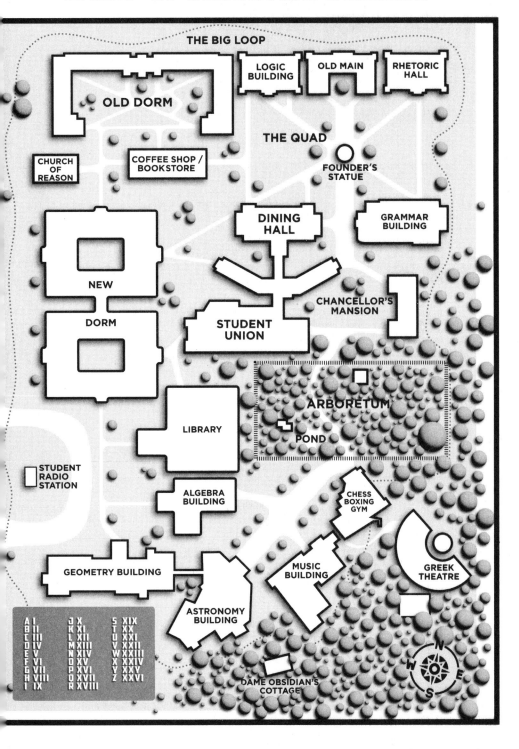

1. THE CASE OF THE INTERRUPTED TOUR

As Freshman Logico took his orientation tour around Deduction College, he gazed at the ivy-covered stone buildings, the statues in the quad, and—a dead body?! That wasn't supposed to be part of the tour, and Logico wanted to make a good impression, so he tried to solve the case.

SUSPECTS

CHANCELLOR OAK

He's a big old walrus-mustached man who wears tweed coats and talks about paradoxes for hours on end. He can show anybody how it all makes sense.

5'5" • LEFT-HANDED • GREEN EYES • GRAY HAIR

RICH KID CHAMPAGNE

He loves his parents' money, but he wishes there was a way to feel morally superior to it. Hopefully, he'll find that in college.

5'11" • LEFT-HANDED • HAZEL EYES • BLOND HAIR

PARTYBOY MANGO

He's ready to party hard and do nothing else, and nothing else is going to keep him from doing nothing else.

5'10" • LEFT-HANDED • BROWN EYES • BROWN HAIR

LOCATIONS

THE QUAD
OUTDOORS

It features a beautiful grass lawn, a fountain, and a great statue of Founder Graystone.

OLD MAIN
INDOORS

This used to be the only building on campus. Now, it's the oldest.

THE COMBINATION COFFEE SHOP/ BOOKSTORE
INDOORS

The only thing that costs more than their textbooks are their lattes.

WEAPONS

A BEAUTIFUL SCHOOL SCARF
MEDIUM-WEIGHT

It's in the official school colors, black and white, chosen because logic is black and white.

A STUFFED PENGUIN
MEDIUM-WEIGHT

The college mascot, because penguins are formal, just like logic.

A HEAVY TOME
HEAVY-WEIGHT

Don't get too excited: it doesn't reveal the mysteries of the universe, just the accounting for the school.

CLUES & EVIDENCE

- Rich Kid Champagne was seen sipping a latte that was more expensive than a textbook.

- The heavy tome was at the northernmost location. (See Exhibit A.)

- The combination coffee shop/bookstore also sold stuffed animals of the school's mascot.

- For once, Chancellor Oak did not have his typical school scarf.

- **The tour was interrupted when they discovered a body at the base of a statue.**

SUSPECTS LOCATIONS

WEAPONS

LOCATIONS

WHO?

WHAT?

WHERE?

2. THE DORMITORY OF DEATH

When Logico arrived at his dormitory, he was stunned by its beauty. It was like a cross between a Spanish castle and a French villa. Now, he had two mysteries to solve: how the school could afford this kind of construction, and who murdered the check-in staff.

SUSPECTS

YOUNG LADY VIOLET

She's practically royalty where she's from: the far-off Holy Nation of Drakonia, although she will modestly insist that she is technically just nobility.

5'0" • RIGHT-HANDED • BLUE EYES • BLOND HAIR

SHY ABALONE

She is incredibly shy, and she hides her face behind her hair. But is she hiding secrets, as well? Or is it just generalized anxiety?

5'6" • RIGHT-HANDED • HAZEL EYES • RED HAIR

WHIZ-KID NIGHT

They're a whiz with numbers. They're a whiz with anything, for that matter. It's almost like magic.

5'9" • LEFT-HANDED • BLUE EYES • BROWN HAIR

LOCATIONS

THE STUDY ROOM
INDOORS

Nobody breaks the silence. In fact, if you do, you might get murdered.

THE GAME ROOM
INDOORS

This place is packed with chessboards. It would be easy for an intense game to end in murder.

THE CAFETERIA
INDOORS

The food is actually surprisingly good, but the meal plan is also surprisingly expensive.

WEAPONS

A RUBY PIN
LIGHT-WEIGHT

Wow, look at that, this ruby pin is really fancy, and it looks expensive!

BOXING GLOVES
MEDIUM-WEIGHT

Use these for chess-boxing, which combines the logic of chess with getting punched in the face.

A LOGIC TEXT-BOOK
MEDIUM-WEIGHT

Every freshman is required to buy this textbook. So logically, it costs a fortune.

CLUES & EVIDENCE

- Shy Abalone was using boxing gloves to cover her face. More shyness? Or was she just using good boxing form?

- Whiz-Kid Night didn't need to buy a copy of the logic textbook because they had memorized it years ago.

- A ruby pin was beside a plate of surprisingly expensive food.

- The shortest suspect was not in the study room.

- **The student's body was found next to a bunch of chessboards.**

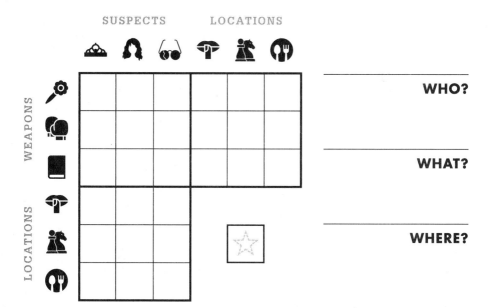

WHO?

WHAT?

WHERE?

3. A LOCKED DORM MYSTERY

Logico was amazed by his room: for one, it was beautiful and spacious, more like a chateau than the cell he'd expected. For two, there was a dead body in the middle of it. Since the door was locked from the inside, one of his roommates must have done it.

SUSPECTS

STRAIGHT-A CRIMSON

She has the best grades in school. But who will she grow up to be? A medical doctor or a political radical? Only time will tell. (But can you guess?)

5'9" • LEFT-HANDED • GREEN EYES • RED HAIR

CHEATER RULEAN

Like Straight-A Crimson, he got a perfect score on his entrance exams. (He also sat behind her.)

5'8" • RIGHT-HANDED • BLUE EYES • RED HAIR

RICH KID CHAMPAGNE

He loves his parents' money, but he wishes there was a way to feel morally superior to it. Hopefully, he'll find that in college.

5'11" • LEFT-HANDED • HAZEL EYES • BLOND HAIR

LOCATIONS

THE BEDROOM COMPLEX
INDOORS

Each of the students has their own room with a desk and an ivy-covered window.

THE COMMON AREA
INDOORS

Over the course of the year, this room will be filled with junk. But for now, it's spotless.

THE BATHROOM
INDOORS

Deduction College sure knows how to spare no expense: the toilets are marble!

WEAPONS

A POISONED TEXTBOOK
MEDIUM-WEIGHT

The ink is poisoned. Fortunately, the book is *The History of Accounting*, so it's unlikely to be read.

A KILLER SNAKE
MEDIUM-WEIGHT

It's easy to train them to kill. It's harder to train them to be sneaky about it.

AN ICE DAGGER
HEAVY-WEIGHT

A classic in locked-room mysteries. The only trace it'll leave behind is a puddle.

CLUES & EVIDENCE

- The tallest suspect was not in the later-to-be-junk-filled room.

- Rich Kid Champagne was standing in a puddle.

- Cheater Rulean side-eyed the person who brought a poisoned textbook. Studying was no way to get good grades in college.

- Whoever was looking out an ivy-covered window was right-handed.

- **Two bites were in the roommate's neck, and a snakeskin was beside the body.**

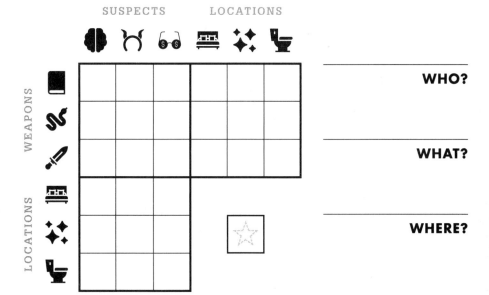

4. OLD MAIN, NEW CORPSE

Freshman Logico was taking several of his classes at Old Main, which was full of history. It was in this very building that Lord Graystone taught the first classes so many years ago. Even today, important things were happening here. Like just before class, Logico's professor had been murdered.

SUSPECTS

COMPUTER NERD INDIGO

Eventually, he will be a rich and famous jerk. Currently, he's just a jerk. But admittedly, he does know a thing or two about computers. (Mostly how to pay people to fix them.)

5'11" • RIGHT-HANDED • GREEN EYES • BROWN HAIR

CHANCELLOR OAK

His lectures go on forever, and he's constantly clearing his throat. Nevertheless, he's mesmerizing. He has a way of making things—like he often says—"just make sense."

5'5" • LEFT-HANDED • GREEN EYES • GRAY HAIR

ASSISTANT PROFESSOR TUSCANY

As a teacher, she is one of the most well-loved and the least well-paid. (The administration argues that the love constitutes a large part of her salary.)

5'5" • LEFT-HANDED • GREEN EYES • BLOND HAIR

LOCATIONS

THE GRAND STEPS
OUTDOORS

Giant steps that lead up to the entrance hall. This is on all the Deduction College postcards.

THE BELL TOWER
INDOORS

It rings twice a day: once at noon and once at twice three till four minus five times six.

THE CHANCELLOR'S OFFICE
INDOORS

Everything in here is made of books, including the desk.

WEAPONS

AN IVORY SCEPTER
HEAVY-WEIGHT

This plays an important part in the graduation ceremonies. It's worth its weight in ivory.

A COURSE CATALOGUE
HEAVY-WEIGHT

A brief description of all the classes at Deduction College. (See Appendix A.)

AN OLD THESIS
MEDIUM-WEIGHT

It argues, quite confusedly, that systemic structures are manifesting the will of their leaders.

CLUES & EVIDENCE

- Chancellor Oak was seen beside a postcard-worthy sight.

- Computer Nerd Indigo had been talking a lot with the person who had the course catalogue.

- A blond suspect was in the location studied in MSC 244, one of the many courses you can take at Deduction College.

- Assistant Professor Tuscany had a medium-weight weapon.

- **A bloodied ivory scepter was found beside the former professor.**

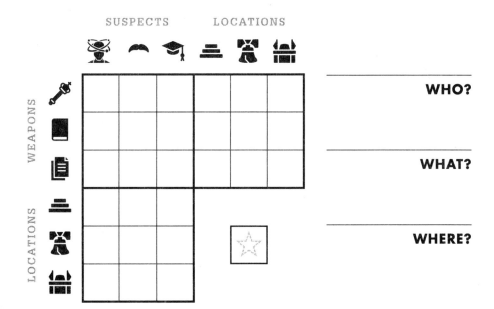

5. DEATH ON THE QUAD

Walking through the quad between classes, Logico caught a glimpse of another ruby pin. However, he didn't see who was wearing it. What he did see, however, was the school chessboxing coach, dead on the quad.

SUSPECTS

STUDENT PRESIDENT PINE

She has one of the sharpest minds in the school, and she knows it. In fact, she could probably kill someone and get away with it. Not that she would, just, you know, she could.

5'6" • RIGHT-HANDED • BROWN EYES • BLACK HAIR

THE MYSTERY BOY

He was wearing an amazingly well-tailored black wool jacket, and he had the most unbelievable hair and piercing emerald eyes.

6'2" • LEFT-HANDED • EMERALD-GREEN EYES • GREAT BROWN HAIR

TRAILBLAZER TANGERINE

They have the goal to be the first nonbinary student to graduate Deduction College. They'll either succeed, or kill trying!

5'5" • LEFT-HANDED • HAZEL EYES • BLOND HAIR

LOCATIONS

THE STATUE OF LORD GRAYSTONE
OUTDOORS

Logico is confused by all the Roman numerals on the base of this statue.

THE FOUNTAIN
OUTDOORS

Precisely calculating the volume of water in the fountain is a common freshman exercise.

THE BIG LAWN
OUTDOORS

This is a perfect place to work on a puzzle book, practice your chessboxing, or . . . murder?!

WEAPONS

A HUNDRED-DOLLAR YO-YO
LIGHT-WEIGHT

A lot more impressive than it sounds because a hundred dollars was a fortune back then.

A GENERIC FLYING DISC
MEDIUM-WEIGHT

This is absolutely not the trademark-protected brand-name toy. No. Totally unrelated.

A RUBY PIN
LIGHT-WEIGHT

These have to represent something. Something secretive, probably.

CLUES & EVIDENCE

- Someone was working through a common freshman exercise with their dominant left hand.

- Logico saw the ruby pin in a perfect place to practice your chessboxing.

- The Mystery Boy rolled his eyes at the person with the generic flying disc.

- Whoever had a weapon worth a fortune was XVIII IX VII VIII XX VIII I XIV IV V IV. (See Exhibit A.)

- **The body was found by the statue of Lord Graystone.**

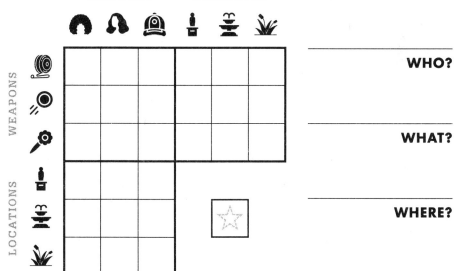

SUSPECTS   LOCATIONS

WHO?

WHAT?

WHERE?

6. THE OPENING POSITION OF THE BODY

Assistant Coach Raspberry walked Logico to the chessboxing gym, spending the entire time telling him how great it was and how much he was going to enjoy it. But when they arrived, Logico learned the dark side of chessboxing: sometimes, one of the chessboxers gets murdered.

SUSPECTS

PRODIGY ROSE

He was a great chess champion as a child. But honestly, at this point, he's a little old to be calling himself a prodigy.

5'7" • LEFT-HANDED • BROWN EYES • BROWN HAIR

ASSISTANT COACH RASPBERRY

He's trying to turn a losing team around, but he's not doing well. You might not know this, but in the coaching community, it's usually considered pretty bad if one of your players is murdered.

6'0" • LEFT-HANDED • BLUE EYES • BLOND HAIR

CHAMPION GOLD

The reigning chessboxing world champion. He's come to show the students a couple of pointers, like his signature method of avoiding wild haymakers.

6'2" • RIGHT-HANDED • BROWN EYES • BROWN HAIR

LOCATIONS

THE LOCKER ROOM
INDOORS

Look, I'm going to be honest with you. It doesn't smell great in here.

THE BOXING RING
INDOORS

Where the result of the match will be determined, either by checkmate or knockout or by the judges.

THE CHESS CLASSROOM
INDOORS

Where you can learn how to move the pieces and everything else you need to know.

WEAPONS

A GIANT KNIGHT
HEAVY-WEIGHT

It's a giant statue of a chess knight that helps with school spirit (and murdering people).

BOXING GLOVES
HEAVY-WEIGHT

Are they supposed to clang when you hit them together?

A CALCULATOR WATCH
LIGHT-WEIGHT

When you want to look smart and sexy . . . you shouldn't get this.

CLUES & EVIDENCE

- The child chess champion was castling in the chess classroom. (Say that three times fast.)

- A suspect with brown eyes was where the result of the match would be determined.

- Whoever had the weapon that helps with school spirit was left-handed.

- A calculator watch was discovered in a not-great-smelling room.

- **Boxing gloves were used to commit the crime.**

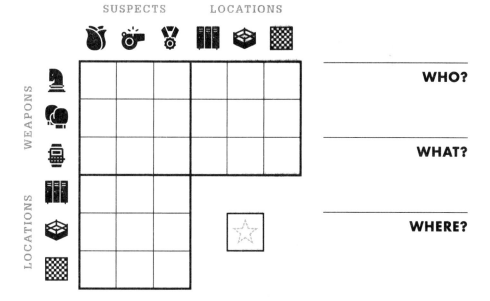

WHO?

WHAT?

WHERE?

7. THE CHANCELLOR'S CLASSIC MANSION MURDER

Crack—boom! Freshman Logico was summoned to the chancellor's mansion to receive a commendation for all the murders he had solved. But when he was walking there, it was pouring rain, and when he arrived, the last student to receive it had been murdered.

SUSPECTS

CHANCELLOR OAK

Nobody on campus has ever heard of a single instance where Chancellor Oak was wrong. Or, at least, where he couldn't convince you he was right.

5'5" • LEFT-HANDED • GREEN EYES • GRAY HAIR

ASSISTANT PROFESSOR TUSCANY

As a teacher, she is one of the least well-paid and the most well-loved.

5'5" • LEFT-HANDED • GREEN EYES • BLOND HAIR

DEAN CELADON

She is an up-and-coming lawyer, ambassador, and idealist, who hopes to never have to murder someone with her bare hands.

5'6" • LEFT-HANDED • GREEN EYES • BROWN HAIR

LOCATIONS

THE BOOK-FILLED LIBRARY
INDOORS

A lot of the books are actually missing from this library, or at least the expensive ones.

THE ENORMOUS DINING HALL
INDOORS

That's interesting, a bunch of the ceramic plates seem to be plastic . . .

THE UNBELIEV-ABLE BALCONY
OUTDOORS

It has an unbelievable view of the campus at night.

WEAPONS

A HEAVY COAT
HEAVY-WEIGHT

The textured fabric is so soft that if you were suffocated with this coat you'd still love it.

A SILVER SILVERWARE SET
HEAVY-WEIGHT

Enough knives and forks to kill someone and still eat your meal.

A PRICELESS VASE
HEAVY-WEIGHT

Ironically, the more expensive something is, the more likely it'll be called priceless.

CLUES & EVIDENCE

- A bunch of knives and forks could be seen from campus (if you had good eyesight).

- Dean Celadon brought a weapon that could suffocate herself—or someone else!

- Because he wasn't wet, Chancellor Oak had obviously been inside the whole time.

- A priceless vase was found where I II XV XV XI XXI XIX V IV XX XV II V. (See Exhibit A.)

- **The murder took place in the dining hall.**

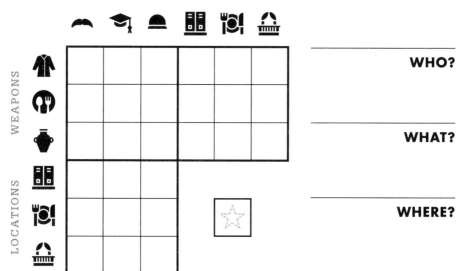

WHO?

WHAT?

WHERE?

8. THE COMBINATION COFFEE SHOP/BOOKSTORE KILLER

Later that week, the newly minted Fellow Logico was getting a cup of coffee and telling the story of what happened at the mansion when he saw the Mystery Boy he had tailed perusing the books. He lost his concentration, and then, there was a scream. A bookseller had been murdered!

SUSPECTS

COFFEE SHOP CHALK

He's really making money on this combination coffee shop/bookstore idea, but he blames his prices on the increasing fees he pays to the college.

5'9" • RIGHT-HANDED • BLUE EYES • BLOND HAIR

CADET COFFEE

This kid is rising through the ranks (of the campus army club), quite possibly because of the sheer amount of coffee he's drinking. He drank his first cup six months ago and now he's up to six a day.

6'0" • RIGHT-HANDED • BROWN EYES • A WISP OF BROWN HAIR

THE MYSTERY BOY

Logico didn't get his name. But he was definitely here. Moseying suspiciously . . .

6'2" • LEFT-HANDED • EMERALD-GREEN EYES • GREAT BROWN HAIR

LOCATIONS

THE TEXTBOOK SECTION
INDOORS

The prices are one of the few things on campus that seem wholly divorced from reason.

THE OUTDOOR DISPLAY
OUTDOORS

Some of their bestselling books are sold out here, like Dame Obsidian's whodunits.

THE COFFEE BAR
INDOORS

The price of a cup of coffee seems reasonable, but only in comparison with the books.

WEAPONS

A GLUTEN-FREE BAGEL
LIGHT-WEIGHT

How could this kill? I'll tell you how—it's actually filled with gluten.

A POT OF BOIL- ING WATER
MEDIUM-WEIGHT

Forget slasher movies. If this is the weapon, it's a splasher film.

A TEXTBOOK ON THE TRIVIUM
HEAVY-WEIGHT

Logic, rhetoric, and grammar are what all freshmen study, if they can afford this book!

CLUES & EVIDENCE

- Green eyes greedily beheld all the textbooks in the textbook section.

- The Mystery Boy ate a gluten-free bagel. Thankfully he didn't actually have a gluten intolerance.

- A trusted friend passed Logico a torn-up napkin he tried to reassemble: EFCSPOEHOF ACKLH ADH A KOXTEBTO.

- The outdoor display was soaked with boiling water.

- **A pot of boiling water was found beside the bookseller.**

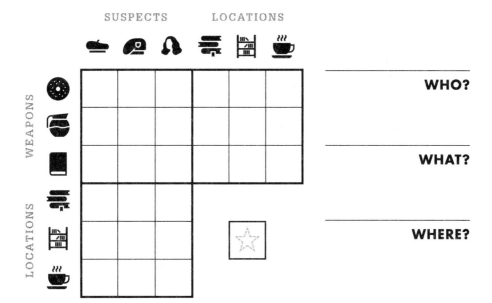

9. DEATH ON THE COUNCIL OF DEANS

Assistant Professor Tuscany brought Freshman Logico before the Council of Deans, and she addressed them, "Great deans! The number of murders that this student has solved is too great!" One of the deans opened their mouth to reply, and then collapsed to the floor.

SUSPECTS

DEAN CELADON

Dean Celadon was definitely going to be expelled from the Council of Deans, but the formal item hadn't officially been added to the agenda yet.

5'6" • LEFT-HANDED • GREEN EYES • BROWN HAIR

ASSISTANT PROFESSOR TUSCANY

She is really becoming Logico's number-one supporter. The stress of it has made her hair go gray.

5'5" • LEFT-HANDED • GREEN EYES • GRAY HAIR

DEAN GLAUCOUS

He had finally made the Council of Deans, and he wasn't going to blow it. Would he have murdered someone over that? Maybe. Probably. (Definitely.)

5'6" • RIGHT-HANDED • BROWN EYES • BROWN HAIR

LOCATIONS

THE ENTRANCE ARCHWAY

INDOORS

Walking through this archway is the dream of every vice dean everywhere.

THE GIANT WINDOW

INDOORS

This is a perfect window for gazing out of ponderously. And it's lined with musty old books!

THE TABLE OF DEANS

INDOORS

It's a round table so that none of the deans is superior to any other.

WEAPONS

A FRAMED DIPLOMA
HEAVY-WEIGHT

This one says that its recipient graduated with a minor in lucky guessing.

A RUBY PIN
LIGHT-WEIGHT

There is definitely some special significance to these ruby pins. But what is it?

A LETTER OPENER
LIGHT-WEIGHT

It opens letters, but it could open arteries just as well.

CLUES & EVIDENCE

- Dean Celadon was not gazing out the window ponderously.

- The shortest suspect was able to stand beneath the entrance archway without ducking.

- Brown eyes were reflected in a ruby. Or maybe a ruby was reflected in brown eyes. However you say it, they were real close to each other.

- Logico's number-one supporter had a weapon that could cut arteries.

- **A shattered diploma was found beside the victim.**

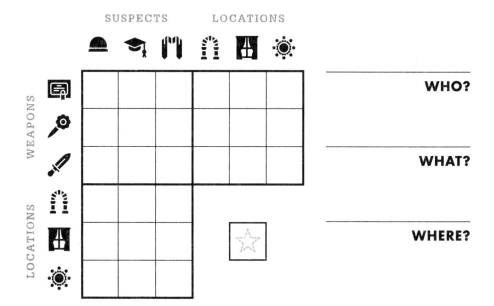

10. BIG CORPSE ON CAMPUS

Deductive Logico stormed into the chancellor's office with the Council of Deans, and he announced that the murders that had been committed this year were actually all connected. And one person was behind it all, using a weapon to arrange all the murders.

SUSPECTS

ASSISTANT COACH RASPBERRY

Sure, he's turning this chessboxing team around. But is he murdering to do it? Or maybe he's just killed a bunch of people so that he can be cut loose of his contract.

6'0" • LEFT-HANDED • BLUE EYES • BLOND HAIR

CHANCELLOR OAK

He has a laugh that people can hear from miles away, especially if what he's laughing at is the poor logic of his conversational partner. Honestly, he's a lot more likely to be murdered than to murder.

5'5" • LEFT-HANDED • GREEN EYES • GRAY HAIR

DEAN GLAUCOUS

There was something in his eyes. Something that suggested he might not be willing to let an opportunity pass him by. That if he needed to do something, he would.

5'6" • RIGHT-HANDED • BROWN EYES • BROWN HAIR

ASSISTANT PROFESSOR TUSCANY

She was certain that she knew what was going to happen next. But it turns out, she didn't know at all.

5'5" • LEFT-HANDED • GREEN EYES • GRAY HAIR

LOCATIONS

THE ARBORETUM
OUTDOORS

This used to be the best place on campus to hang out. Now, honestly? It's the worst.

OLD MAIN
INDOORS

Emphasis on the "old." This building is full of history and asbestos.

THE CHANCELLOR'S MANSION
INDOORS

This is rented to the chancellor for $1 a year, and he's still refusing to pay.

THE CHESSBOXING GYM
INDOORS

They haven't won in ten years. According to the Lindy effect, they won't win for ten more.

WEAPONS

AN OLD COMPUTER
HEAVY-WEIGHT

Hey, if it ain't broke . . . it will be when you kill someone with it.

A HEAVY THESIS
HEAVY-WEIGHT

A thesis on how economic instability can compound self-destructive behavior.

A FRAMED DIPLOMA
HEAVY-WEIGHT

A Deduction College diploma is worth a lot. Maybe not what you pay for it, but a lot.

THE POWER OF LOGIC ITSELF
SORTA EPHEMERAL

If you have the power of logic, you do not need a weapon to kill. You can just convince them to die.

MOTIVES

 TO MAKE THE CHESSBOXING TEAM WIN AGAIN

 TO TAKE OVER THE SCHOOL

 TO KEEP THEIR JOB

 TO AVOID ADMITTING THEY WERE WRONG

CLUES & EVIDENCE

- The old computer still ran: that meant that it was not left outdoors.

- If Assistant Professor Tuscany would kill, then she would do it to take over the school.

- The person who wielded the power of logic was not an assistant anything.

- Nowhere else on campus was more the home of the power of logic itself than the Chancellor's Mansion.

- Assistant Coach Raspberry would do anything he could in order to make the chessboxing team a winning team again.

- The heavy thesis was in a building filled with asbestos.

- Assistant Coach Raspberry was in the building directly south of the arboretum. (See Exhibit A.)

- Chancellor Oak would do anything to avoid admitting he was wrong . . . even kill!

- Dean Glaucous was seen wandering the arboretum, despite the clearly posted signs advertising its danger.

- **These crimes were committed with the power of logic itself.**

SUSPECTS   MOTIVES   LOCATIONS

WEAPONS

LOCATIONS

MOTIVES

WHO?

WHAT?

WHERE?

WHY?

SOPHOMORE

Oh muse, sing to me!

—Homer, *The Odyssey*

After a disastrous year, the Council of Deans spent a lot of time talking about how to reform their school and break with the policies of the disgraced Chancellor Oak, specifically his policy of losing a lot of money for the school.

They tried to trim costs as best as they could, but cutting expenses is never fun. So instead, they tried to come up with ways to increase revenue for the school, as well. After minutes of thought (which they would later claim was hours, and after that, days), they hit upon a wonderful idea.

In a blatant attempt at good old distraction publicity, the up-and-coming mystery writer Dame Obsidian was invited to live on campus all semester as a visiting lecturer and artist in residence, and her class (tentatively titled "The Logic of the Mystery") was already filling up.

"Didn't she murder her husband?" Sophomore Logico asked, referring to the book she had recently published: *How I Murdered My Husband: An Idunit.*

"That's just a novel!" Logico's classmate Whiz-Kid Night interjected. "You don't believe that just because someone writes about murder, they must have committed it, do you?"

"But didn't her husband go missing around the same time?" Logico asked.

His questions were received only by embarrassed chuckles, as if he just didn't understand art. So, he decided he would apply for the class.

Not only was he interested in learning about the topic, but he was also interested in keeping an eye on Dame Obsidian. (Also, he saw the Mystery Boy applying.)

Unfortunately, competition for spots was fierce, and there was absolutely no guarantee. But Logico was not deterred. He would figure out a way to convince her to admit him if it was the last thing he did.

(And, considering her reputation, it might be!)

THE (UN)STAINED GLASS WINDOW

11. MURDER IS A COTTAGE INDUSTRY

Deductive Logico desperately wanted to be admitted to Dame Obsidian's class, so he brought a bouquet of flowers to the cottage that the college had loaned her. He knocked, and she answered, but before he could ask her about her class, she asked him to solve a murder committed right there in her cottage.

SUSPECTS

DAME OBSIDIAN

Today's lecture notes involve how to hide a good clue in plain sight and also how to stab someone the "right" way. ("In fiction, of course," she says, but then she winks!)

5'4" • LEFT-HANDED • GREEN EYES • BLACK HAIR

FAN FICCER PEARL

She's shipping two of the other students in class in a lemon fic she's writing. It's . . . actually great.

5'5" • RIGHT-HANDED • BLUE EYES • BLOND HAIR

MFA CANDIDATE GAINSBORO

He's got a million notes on your story, and the biggest one is that he hates it.

6'0" • LEFT-HANDED • HAZEL EYES • BROWN HAIR

LOCATIONS

HER WRITING DESK
INDOORS

Where Dame Obsidian plans her next murder. Her next fictional murder, of course!

HER BOOKSHELVES
INDOORS

Filled with the dame's own books in dozens of different languages. What is that dirt?

HER BALCONY
OUTDOORS

For looking out over the town, or establishing an alibi by waving at people.

WEAPONS

HOW I MURDERED MY HUSBAND
MEDIUM-WEIGHT

Dame Obsidian's bestselling (and completely fictional) story about how she killed her husband.

AN OLD-TIMEY TYPEWRITER
HEAVY-WEIGHT

With this, Dame Obsidian has written all of her murders and committed several of them.

A CAN OF GRAY PAINT
MEDIUM-WEIGHT

To Logico, this is a very reasonable color of paint. But it's certainly not very expressive.

CLUES & EVIDENCE

- Fan Ficcer Pearl was seen hanging around next to Dame Obsidian's writing desk.

- A can of gray paint was outdoors. What had it been used for?

- The suspect with a million notes had a medium-weight weapon.

- Dame Obsidian didn't need to read her own books, so she never visited her bookshelves.

- **A bestselling (and completely fictional!) book was used to commit the crime.**

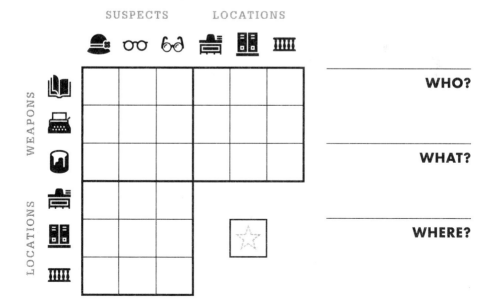

12. THE IMPOSSIBLE CHAPEL MURDER

On the night before the beginning of senior year, there was an impossible murder on campus. The Church of Reason was the site of the brutal murder, and the giant doors had been locked from the outside. By the next morning, everyone on campus knew the facts.

SUSPECTS

FRAT BRO BROWNSTONE

A fraternity bro who worships the party and the thrill of the chug. No matter what happens, he's never gonna stop partying!

5'4" • LEFT-HANDED • BROWN EYES • BROWN HAIR

SORORITY SISTER LAPIS

She loves being in a sisterhood, and she never wants it to end.

5'2" • RIGHT-HANDED • BROWN EYES • BROWN HAIR

NOBODY

There were only two people in the chapel. So nobody was in the third location.

LOCATIONS

THE NONDENOMI-NATIONAL ALTAR
INDOORS

There's an altar and a statue with a sword that is labeled secularly.

THE FUNCTIONAL PEWS
INDOORS

They're gray cement (for neutrality), but they're actually very, very comfortable.

THE (UN) STAINED GLASS WINDOW
INDOORS

The most beautiful uncolored, nondenominational art you've ever seen. (See Exhibit B.)

WEAPONS

A HYMNAL
MEDIUM-WEIGHT

These are mostly just pop songs, so everyone can enjoy them.

A BOTTLE OF OIL
LIGHT-WEIGHT

It's a bottle of cooking oil, which, for many people, is the most sacred oil of all.

A BOTTLE OF WINE
MEDIUM-WEIGHT

Drinking booze is not just a religious thing. It's for everyone.

CLUES & EVIDENCE

- A drink for everyone was found on gray cement.

- Sorority Sister Lapis was a huge fan of pop songs and carried them with her.

- Somebody (not nobody) was sitting on a pew.

- If, in the (un)stained glass window, you colored the Vs and Cs yellow, and the Ts and Zs red, you'd see an image of the weapon that was closest to the (un)stained glass. (See Exhibit B.)

- **The body was found on the nondenominational altar.**

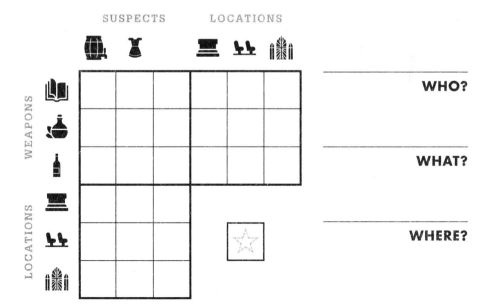

13. OVERGROWN AND AFTERLIFE

Sophomore Logico went for a stroll through the campus arboretum, which had long ago become an overgrown tangle of trees, weeds, and vines. A big sign was posted that read DANGER: DON'T GO OFF TRAIL. Logico ignored that sign and got lost in the darkness. Then, he heard a scream. Then, he found a body. Should've obeyed the sign . . .

SUSPECTS

LONER SNOW

He just wants to be by himself, all alone. Argh, why won't you just leave him alone?!

6'3" • RIGHT-HANDED • GRAY EYES • WHITE HAIR

WHIZ-KID NIGHT

Why would a math nerd be out in the overgrown arboretum? They say it's because numbers underlie all of reality, constituting the fundamental substrate of existence. But do you actually believe that?

5'9" • LEFT-HANDED • BLUE EYES • BROWN HAIR

BOTANIST ONYX

She is studying a bunch of new plants that she's found.

5'0" • RIGHT-HANDED • BROWN EYES • BLACK HAIR

LOCATIONS

THE HIDDEN POND
OUTDOORS

In the daytime, this is probably a romantic spot. At nighttime . . . did you hear that?

THE RUSTED GATE
OUTDOORS

The metal letters are covered in moss, but they seem to read ENTER.

THE MYSTERIOUS BUILDING
OUTDOORS

This is a strange structure that is covered with leaves and vines. What could it be?

WEAPONS

A MACHETE	A FLAME-THROWER	A CARNIVOROUS PLANT
HEAVY-WEIGHT	HEAVY-WEIGHT	MEDIUM-WEIGHT
You don't have to explain how this is a weapon. You have to explain how it's not!	Honestly, maybe the best way to get rid of all this overgrowth.	This is probably not big enough to eat a person. But the pot it's in could kill them.

CLUES & EVIDENCE

- You can see an image of the weapon beside the hidden pond if, in the (un)stained glass window, you colored the Ss and Bs green, the Ps and Ks brown, and the F red. (See Exhibit B.)

- A machete was found next to a vine-covered structure.

- In an amazing piece of detective work, Logico found a single brown hair by the mysterious building.

- Botanist Onyx was afraid of the person who brought a flamethrower.

- **The body was draped over the rusted gate.**

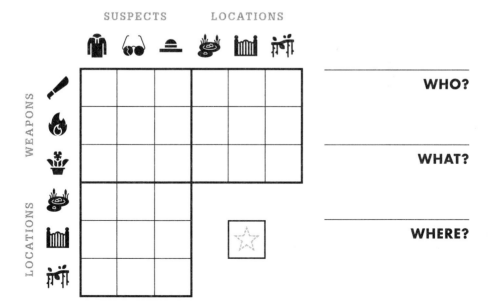

14. EXTRA! EXTRA! THE EDITOR'S DEAD!

Dame Obsidian wrote an article in the school paper reassuring the students she wasn't going to murder anyone (see Appendix B), but when they didn't print it right away, she asked Logico to look into it. When he did, he discovered a good reason they hadn't printed her article: the editor of the newspaper was dead!

SUSPECTS

JUNIOR EDITOR IVORY

She's a great junior editor of the student newspaper. She introduced the campus gossip column, which is currently its most popular section.

5'6" • LEFT-HANDED • BROWN EYES • BROWN HAIR

FOREIGN-EXCHANGE RED

He has started an extracurricular war reenactment club, except that the war they're supposedly reenacting is the future revolution in Drakonia.

6'2" • LEFT-HANDED • BROWN EYES • BROWN HAIR

PHOTOGRAPHER DUSTY

He's going to be a great art photographer one day, not some sellout film director. (And no, he won't photograph your event.)

5'10" • LEFT-HANDED • HAZEL EYES • BALD

LOCATIONS

THE BULLPEN
INDOORS

At least, that's what the real newsrooms call 'em. It's where the writers write/argue.

THE EDITOR'S OFFICE
INDOORS

Where the real work gets done, mostly by telling other people to do the actual work.

THE STORAGE ROOM
INDOORS

It's filled with old yearbooks, old newspapers, and old mice.

WEAPONS

A SACK FULL OF METAL LETTERS
HEAVY-WEIGHT

They used to print the paper with these. Now, they're just used for murder.

THE CLASSIC NEWSPAPER-WRAPPED CROWBAR
MEDIUM-WEIGHT

This is the first time this now-classic was ever used.

A FAKE ASPIRATIONAL BOOKIE
MEDIUM-WEIGHT

A plastic replica of the prestigious Bookerman Prize.

CLUES & EVIDENCE

- The suspect with an extracurricular reenactment club had a sack full of metal letters.

- A plastic replica was found in the editor's office.

- Photographer Dusty was afraid of mice and would never go near one.

- Junior Editor Ivory hated the person who brought the original of the now-classic.

- **The senior editor's body was found in the bullpen.**

SUSPECTS   LOCATIONS

WEAPONS

LOCATIONS

WHO?

WHAT?

WHERE?

15. THE MID-GAME MURDER

As a sophomore, Logico was finally old enough for his first chessboxing match, and he was excited to try his skill on the board and in the ring. Terrifyingly, in the middle of the match, a fan was murdered in the stands! (But luckily for Logico, it kept him from having to fight his first boxing round against Chessboxer Blaze.)

SUSPECTS

THE MYSTERY BOY

He was watching from the stands, and even though he didn't clap or cheer, it is possible that, in some way, he was cheering Logico on, right?

6'2" • LEFT-HANDED • EMERALD-GREEN EYES • GREAT BROWN HAIR

ASTRONOMER AZURE

She loves studying the stars. She thinks there must be something more to them than what is taught in class. But she doesn't think (like her mother, Bishop Azure) that they're dancing angels.

5'6" • RIGHT-HANDED • HAZEL EYES • BROWN HAIR

SORORITY SISTER LAPIS

She likes rooting for the chessboxing team, sure, but not nearly as much as she loves organizing her sorority's end-of-semester theatrical spectaculars.

5'2" • RIGHT-HANDED • BROWN EYES • BROWN HAIR

LOCATIONS

THE CHEAP SEATS
INDOORS

They try to make sure some of the students can afford tickets to these fights.

THE FLOOR SEATS
INDOORS

Seats on the floor of a collegiate intramural fight tournament? You can't imagine the cost.

THE IN-BETWEEN SEATS
INDOORS

Look, most seats aren't the floor seats or the cheap seats. These are those seats.

WEAPONS

A SCHOOL PENNANT LIGHT-WEIGHT	**AN EXPLODING HOT DOG** MEDIUM-WEIGHT	**A BIG FOAM FINGER** LIGHT-WEIGHT
Not sure how a tiny flag could kill somebody, but everyone at DC is really smart.	You don't want to know how the sausage is made (with explosives).	There's actually a spear gun in the index finger.

CLUES & EVIDENCE

- A big foam finger was surprisingly not in the cheap seats.

- The second tallest suspect brought a weapon you could see in the unstained glass window if you stained the Ls and Hs red and the Ps and Ks brown. (See Exhibit B.)

- The suspect in the floor seats watched with green eyes.

- Sorority Sister Lapis thought the person who brought a school pennant was cute.

- **The murdered fan's body was found in the in-between seats . . .**

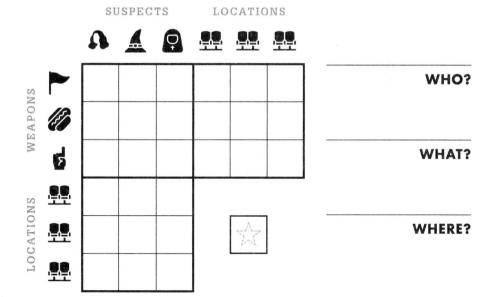

WHO?

WHAT?

WHERE?

16. THE STAYOVER SLAYING

After the match was over, it was time for the winter break. Sophomore Logico decided to stay at the university over the holidays, when it was just him, a few other students, and some lonely professors. But then, on Christmas morning, Logico found a body on campus. At least he had something to do.

SUSPECTS

VICE DEAN TUSCANY

She is spending the entire holiday working tirelessly on the administrative side of the school.

5'5" • LEFT-HANDED • GREEN EYES • GRAY HAIR

THE MYSTERY BOY

Why is he here over the break? His clothes seem too expensive for him not to have somewhere to go. Maybe he just likes studying.

6'2" • LEFT-HANDED • EMERALD-GREEN EYES • GREAT BROWN HAIR

SHY ABALONE

Maybe Shy Abalone isn't shy—maybe she's got no one in her life who loves her . . . because she murdered them!

5'6" • RIGHT-HANDED • HAZEL EYES • RED HAIR

LOCATIONS

THE CHESSBOXING GYM
INDOORS

It was hard to work out with the rest of the team gone. Play both sides? Punch yourself?

THE SILENT ARCHWAY
OUTDOORS

It's bad luck to talk under it, but that rumor was started by an anti-noise professor.

THE QUAD
OUTDOORS

It was strange to see the quad empty and covered in snow, when it was usually so busy.

WEAPONS

A BEAUTIFUL SCARF
MEDIUM-WEIGHT

Ironic that the same scarf could either protect your neck or strangle it.

ANOTHER RUBY PIN
LIGHT-WEIGHT

What the heck is going on with these pins? Logico is going to ask about this.

AN UNOPENED PRESENT
HEAVY-WEIGHT

Is it a set of puzzle books, or a boxing glove on a spring? Only one way to find out.

CLUES & EVIDENCE

- Vice Dean Tuscany was pacing the quad.

- The Mystery Boy was still wearing one of those ruby pins!

- Shy Abalone did not have the weapon you could see in the unstained glass window if you colored the Qs and Js orange and the Ys and Ns red. (See Exhibit B.)

- An unopened present was certainly not under the silent archway.

- **The murder took place in the chessboxing gym.**

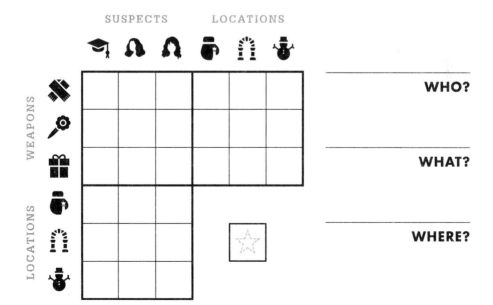

17. WRITING IS MURDER

When school started back up again, Dame Obsidian called a school-wide meeting at the school's commencement hall. She was going to make an announcement revealing the true culprit behind all the murders on campus. However, before she could make her announcement, one of the attendees was murdered.

SUSPECTS

THE INCREDIBLY TALENTED BLACKSTONE

This guy writes the most evocative stories. He is an unbelievable talent who might just change literature as we know it.

6'0" • RIGHT-HANDED • BROWN EYES • A FULL HEAD OF HAIR

WHIZ-KID NIGHT

We were going to print a "fun little mathematical fact" from Whiz-Kid Night in this box. But it was way too long, and also, their definition of "fun" was pretty unique.

5'9" • LEFT-HANDED • BLUE EYES • BROWN HAIR

DAME OBSIDIAN

One of the things that makes some people suspicious about Dame Obsidian murdering people is how often people around her get murdered. Like, all the time.

5'4" • LEFT-HANDED • GREEN EYES • BLACK HAIR

LOCATIONS

THE ENTRANCE
INDOORS

During commencement, passing through it symbolizes you stepping into the ranks of the unemployed.

THE STAGE
INDOORS

There's a podium and a lectern, and the difference between those is one of the many questions on the final exam.

THE SEATS
INDOORS

These seats should probably be a little more comfortable for what the donors paid.

WEAPONS

A MODERN TYPEWRITER
MEDIUM-WEIGHT

To be honest, for what other reason would you bring a typewriter to class except to murder?

A FOUNTAIN PEN
LIGHT-WEIGHT

This pen costs more than your car. And it still leaks ink!

A PIECE OF PAPER
LIGHT-WEIGHT

How would this kill you? It has a spooky message on it that scares you to death.

CLUES & EVIDENCE

- The guy who writes the most evocative stories was not standing beneath the entrance.

- Logico wrote down a clue in his Detective Notebook and then accidentally shredded the page. When he tried to put it back together, it looked like this: A AOITUNNF ENP WSA OTN ON TEH ESAGT.

- Dame Obsidian was carrying a piece of paper she wouldn't read.

- Whiz-Kid Night was sitting in one of the seats.

- **A few broken typewriter keys were found beside the student's body.**

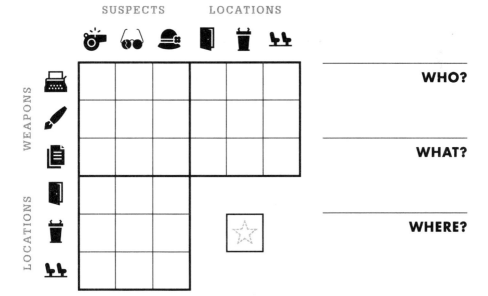

18. BOOK LAUNCH, BODY FALL

Coffee Shop Chalk's combination coffee shop/bookstore was packed with students, faculty, and alumni, excited to hear Dame Obsidian reading from her new book. They wanted to know if there really was someone orchestrating all the recent murders. If there was, they had just orchestrated another one: an Obsidian superfan had been killed.

SUSPECTS

COFFEE SHOP CHALK

He's really making money on this combination coffee shop/bookstore idea, especially since, on a college campus, he can charge anything for both.

5'9" • RIGHT-HANDED • BLUE EYES • WHITE HAIR

THE MYSTERY BOY

Once again, this mystery boy is at the combination coffee shop/bookstore/scene of the crime. That's pretty suspicious, isn't it? But then again, Logico was there both times, too . . .

6'2" • LEFT-HANDED • EMERALD-GREEN EYES • GREAT BROWN HAIR

DAME OBSIDIAN

When Dame Obsidian hears about a particularly clever murder, she frequently expresses admiration for the murderer, saying something like "That's so clever!" or "I wish I'd thought of that."

5'4" • LEFT-HANDED • GREEN EYES • BLACK HAIR

LOCATIONS

THE LINE FOR AUTOGRAPHS
INDOORS

A great scam would be to have a famous author "autograph" some falsified money orders.

THE SIGN OUT FRONT
OUTDOORS

It says, MEET DAME OBSIDIAN! GET HER MOST RECENT BOOK! SAVE YOUR LIFE!

THE CHECKOUT
INDOORS

The only place on campus that collects more money than the alumni donations office.

WEAPONS

A BIG, GIANT SWORD
HEAVY-WEIGHT

It looks like an old-timey religious sword. But I bet it kills secularly, too.

A BUNDLE OF PENCILS
MEDIUM-WEIGHT

Just grab and stab. These #2 pencils are #1 for murder.

DAME OBSIDIAN'S LATEST MASTERPIECE
MEDIUM-WEIGHT

A first edition of her latest book. If it's used to kill, it'll be worth a fortune.

CLUES & EVIDENCE

- Coffee Shop Chalk had one rule: never stand in line for anything, ever. He didn't break it.

- Dame Obsidian was carrying a big, giant sword to fight off any superfans who got too close.

- A really strong, well-conditioned, and healthy head of brown hair was found by the sign out front.

- The Mystery Boy was seen reading Dame Obsidian's latest masterpiece.

- **The body was found at the checkout! They checked out of life . . .**

SUSPECTS   LOCATIONS

WEAPONS

LOCATIONS

WHO?

WHAT?

WHERE?

19. *WHAT HAPPENED AT DEDUCTION COLLEGE: A YOUDUNIT!*

Sophomore Logico started reading Dame Obsidian's novel eagerly. Though her references to real-life campus personalities were thinly veiled, they were not difficult to deduce, and Logico was shocked to discover who she was accusing of committing the crimes.

SUSPECTS

BOY DETECTIVE BLAKENWITTE

Okay, so this character is clearly based on Logico, and honestly it's not flattering at all. He's always right, technically, but in an annoying way.

5'9" • RIGHT-HANDED • BROWN EYES • BLACK HAIR

SUPER SPOOKY SECRETINO

Clearly based on the Mystery Boy. He reads poetry and talks about big tragic things with grand gestures. But do you ever see him do any real work? No! Never.

6'2" • LEFT-HANDED • WEIRD GREEN EYES • OKAY BROWN HAIR

THE ANNOYING CINEREOUS

A lot of people disagree about who this is, but it's really obvious if you think about it.

6'0" • LEFT-HANDED • HAZEL EYES • BROWN HAIR

LOCATIONS

DAME OBSIDIAN'S COTTAGE
INDOORS

Okay, in the book, she depicts herself as living a lot more modestly than she does.

THE CHURCH OF REASON
INDOORS

Another iconic Dame Obsidian location, like the greenhouse where she *didn't* bury her husband.

THE ARBORETUM
OUTDOORS

There's a great scene set here where people keep tripping on roots and the killer gets them.

WEAPONS

A RED HERRING
MEDIUM-WEIGHT

Every Dame Obsidian book has red herrings in it, but this one has a literal one.

A TICKING CLOCK
MEDIUM-WEIGHT

Not only does the plot require the characters to act fast, there's also one of those timed explosives.

STAKES
HEAVY-WEIGHT

Like, the kind where there are consequences for failure, but also the kind you can use to stab people.

CLUES & EVIDENCE

- There's a scene in the book where the Annoying Cinerous keeps tripping on roots until the killer gets them.

- The Boy Detective Blakenwitte did not have a ticking clock.

- If you colored the Ms and Xs red in the (un)stained glass window, you would see the weapon at the cottage. (See Exhibit B.)

- There were stakes in the arboretum. High stakes!

- **Obsidian still has the crime take place in the Church of Reason.**

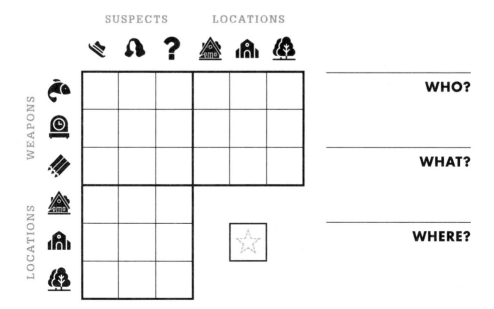

WHO?

WHAT?

WHERE?

20. DEATH AFTER LIFE

Deductive Logico showed up to Dame Obsidian's final class and announced, "Your book is wrong." Obsidian laughed, and then asked him to prove it. "I will! I know who committed the impossible chapel murder!" And he proceeded to explain his case.

SUSPECTS

FRAT BRO BROWNSTONE

A fraternity bro who worships the party and the thrill of the chug. No matter what happens, he's never gonna stop partying!

5'4" • LEFT-HANDED • BROWN EYES • BROWN HAIR

SORORITY SISTER LAPIS

She loves being in a sisterhood, and she never wants it to end.

5'2" • RIGHT-HANDED • BROWN EYES • BROWN HAIR

THE MYSTERY BOY

He was here to clear his name. Whatever his name actually was.

6'2" • LEFT-HANDED • EMERALD-GREEN EYES • GREAT BROWN HAIR

DAME OBSIDIAN

She doesn't like that Logico has interrupted her final class, and in fact, she looks like she's going to murder him over it.

5'4" • LEFT-HANDED • GREEN EYES • BLACK HAIR

LOCATIONS

THE NONDENOMINATIONAL ALTAR
INDOORS

Even for a Church of Reason, committing a murder on top of it feels pretty taboo.

THE FUNCTIONAL PEWS
INDOORS

Logico doubted these gray cement pews, but they're actually quite comfortable for thinking.

THE (UN)STAINED GLASS WINDOW
INDOORS

The light through this window makes everything look, like, totally awesome.

THE FRONT STEPS
OUTDOORS

These beautiful stone steps would be a really epic place to get murdered.

WEAPONS

A HYMNAL
MEDIUM-WEIGHT

These are mostly just pop songs, so everyone can enjoy them.

A BOTTLE OF OIL
LIGHT-WEIGHT

It's a bottle of cooking oil, which, for many people, is the most sacred oil of all.

A BOTTLE OF WINE
MEDIUM-WEIGHT

Drinking booze is not just a religious thing. It's for everyone.

A GIANT SWORD
HEAVY-WEIGHT

Reason will help you win any argument, and this sword is named "Reason."

MODUS OPERANDI (HOW THEY DID IT)

 PAINTING THEMSELVES LIKE A STATUE

 THROUGH A SECRET PASSAGE

 WITH SMOKE AND MIRRORS

 BRO SCIENCE

CLUES & EVIDENCE

- First of all, all the clues we already know are still true, but only the clues themselves, and not the deductions you made from them. (See Case 12: The Impossible Chapel Murder.)

- Gray paint was found at one suspect's house: they could have painted themself gray to disguise themself as a statue. (See Case 11: Murder is a Cottage Industry.)

- Logico was convinced that the suspect who disappeared after the chessboxing coach was murdered would have committed this perfect murder using a secret passageway. (See Case 5: Death on the Quad.)

- One suspect was seen with their weapon at a book launch. (See Case 18: Book Launch, Body Fall.)

- The person with experience organizing end-of-semester theatrical spectaculars would have used smoke and mirrors to perform this impossible crime. (See Case 15: The Mid-Game Murder.)

- What Logico realized is that the Mystery Boy must have seen something while standing outside the chapel.

- **This all explains how the body could be found on the altar!**

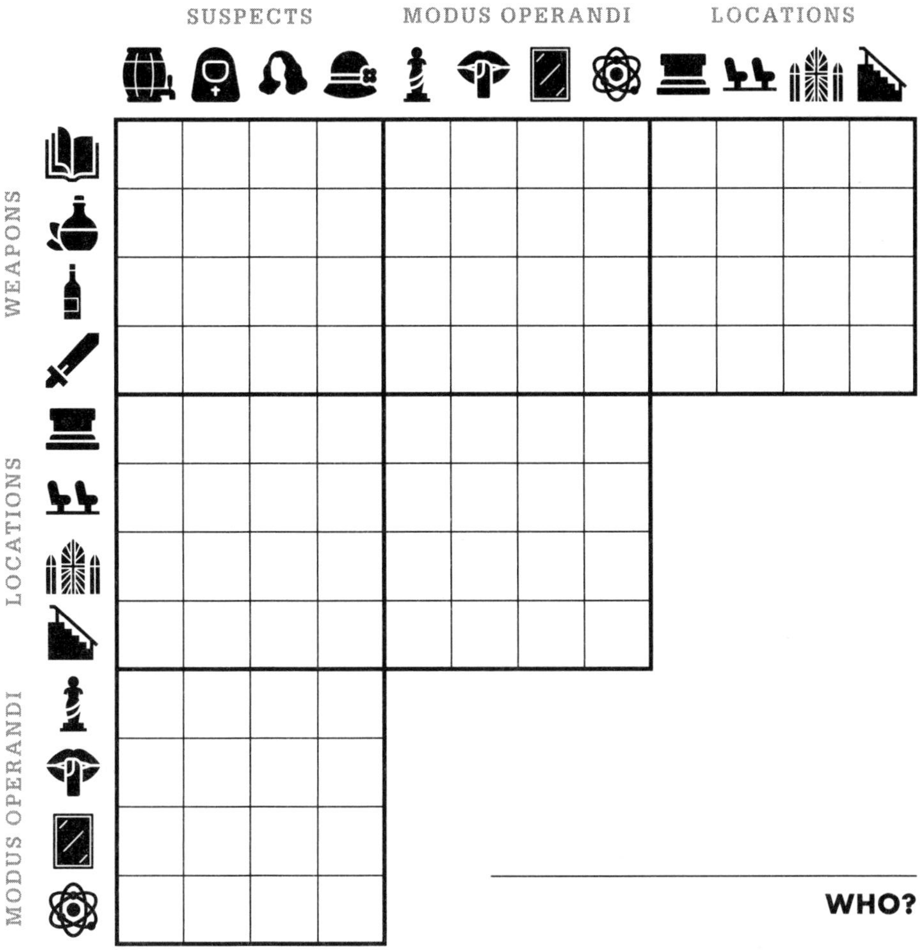

WEAPONS

LOCATIONS

MODUS OPERANDI

WHO?

WHAT?

WHERE?

HOW?

EXHIBIT C

THE PLAQUE ON THE FOUNDER'S STATUE

IX-XXII-XIV-XXII-XIV-XXV-XXII-IX ·
VII-XIX-XXII-VIII-XXII · IV-XII-IX-XXIII-VIII

XXII-V-XXII-IX-II-VII-XIX-XVIII-XIII-XX · XIV-XXVI-II ·
XXV-XXII · XX-IX-XXVI-VIII-XI-XXII-XXIII ·
IV-XVIII-VII-XIX · XV-XII-XX-XVIII-XXIV

XXV-XXVI-XIII-XVIII-VIII-XIX · VII-XIX-XXII ·
XXIII-XXII-XV-VI-VIII-XVIII-XII-XIII · VII-XIX-XXVI-VII

XXII-VIII-XII-VII-XXII-IX-XVIII-XXIV-XVIII-VIII-XIV ·
XIX-XXVI-VIII · XVIII-VII-VIII · XI-XV-XXVI-XXIV-XXIV-XXII

XV-XXII-VII · II-XII-VI-IX-VIII-XXII-XV-XXI · XXV-XXII ·
XIII-XII-VII · XXIII-XXII-XXIV-XXII-XVIII-V-XXII-XXIII

JUNIOR

Humans are by nature political animals.

—Aristotle, *Politics*

This new year was shaping up to be a very special one for Logico, and for Deduction College itself.

For one, the resignation of Student President Pine (on account of being expelled for murder) had left an opening in the campus political scene. Several students were announcing their candidacy for the most powerful position in student government.

But not only that, junior year was the first year where student athletes could play on the varsity chessboxing team. If Logico was strong enough and smart enough (or, if you prefer, lucky enough) to be offered a spot, then there was even a chance that he could travel to the National Collegiate Chessboxing Championship as an official competitor.

One thing that was certain, though, was that there would be more mysteries to solve, more riddles to unravel, and more to learn about Logico's favorite subject: the Mysterious Irratino, who seemed to know much more than he admitted.

In these ten puzzles, you have to solve not only who did it, how, and where—but a fourth element as well. This will vary from case to case, but discovering it will be essential to determining whodunit.

Nevertheless, if these puzzles are still too easy for you, here is an assignment you can solve for extra credit: once again, there is a master manipulator behind the scenes of these murders, and if you can identify it before Logico, you'll earn yourself some gold stars.

Good luck, junior!

21. THE DEAD CAN'T VOTE (OR CAN THEY?)

Since Student President Pine had been expelled, this year her position was up for grabs. On the first day of school, there was a candidate registration drive. Everyone wanted one person to run: she was intelligent, charismatic, and kind. There was only one problem: she was dead. Surely, Logico thought, one of the other candidates did it. But who? And what was their platform?

SUSPECTS

REBEL UMBER

She wants to fight the power and doesn't think there's much value to the electoral system, but she's excellent at theory, and she knows how to read a room.

5'4" • LEFT-HANDED • BLUE EYES • BLOND HAIR

CANDIDATE RED

He has started an extracurricular war reenactment club, except that the war they're reenacting hasn't happened yet.

6'2" • LEFT-HANDED • BROWN EYES • BROWN HAIR

CANDIDATE RULEAN

Candidate Rulean managed to exploit an obscure bylaw in the student government constitution to get his expulsion delayed until after the student body president weighs in on it. Now he just has to get himself elected student body president.

5'8" • RIGHT-HANDED • BLUE EYES • RED HAIR

CANDIDATE HONEY

He's just a regular student who is sick of these political dynasties and wants to see some ordinary folks in government for a change. He loves puppies and all registered voters.

6'0" • LEFT-HANDED • HAZEL EYES • BROWN HAIR

LOCATIONS

A NICE SPOT IN THE GRASS
OUTDOORS

There's a blanket and every-thing. This is a great, romantic spot to cuddle or practice your chessboxing.

A VOTER REGISTRATION TABLE
OUTDOORS

It's weird that they make the students register even though they're all enrolled. Seems like it would disenfranchise people!

THE STATUE OF LORD GRAYSTONE
OUTDOORS

Logico is going to commit him-self to deciphering what the message on the statue says.

THE SIDEWALK
OUTDOORS

They built this sidewalk here because students ruined the grass walking on this exact path.

WEAPON

A COFFEE THERMOS
MEDIUM-WEIGHT • MADE OF PLASTIC & COFFEE

This can keep your coffee warm or make a body cold!

TOO BIG A BITE
MEDIUM-WEIGHT • MADE OF FOOD

Try to eat this in one go and you're likely to choke . . . exactly as planned.

A RUBY PIN
LIGHT-WEIGHT • MADE OF METAL & A GEMSTONE

Honestly, they seem a little dark for rubies. But Logico doesn't know that many gemstones . . .

THE CHESSBOXING CHAMPIONSHIP TROPHY
HEAVY-WEIGHT • MADE OF METAL

The DC won this chessboxing trophy a decade ago, and they haven't won since. Is this the year? (Statistically? No.)

THEIR PLATFORM

 FEWER REQUIRED COURSES

 OVERTURN THE ADMINISTRATION

 MORE LENIENCY FOR MURDERERS

 KEEP THINGS COMFORTABLY AS THEY ARE

CLUES & EVIDENCE

- Either Rebel Umber or Candidate Honey was wearing a ruby pin.

- Whoever was at a nice spot in the grass was right-handed.

- The suspect who wanted to see ordinary folks in office had a coffee thermos.

- The person who wants to fight the power was seen at a voter registration table.

- The person with the championship trophy was campaigning on overturning the school administration entirely.

- The person who was campaigning on keeping things comfortably as they are was not on the sidewalk.

- Whoever was campaigning on more leniency for murderers was right-handed.

- There was no coffee anywhere near the statue of Lord Graystone.

- **Too big a bite was found in the throat of the perfect candidate.**

SUSPECTS   THEIR PLATFORM   LOCATIONS

WEAPONS

LOCATIONS

THEIR PLATFORM

WHO?

WHAT?

WHERE?

AND?

22. A CAMPUS CANVAS KILLER

Candidate Honey was going around campus knocking on doors, making sure he introduced himself to every possible voter. But when he knocked on one of the on-campus doors, instead of a voter, he met a body. Of course he immediately called Logico for help. Everybody now knew to call him in the event of a murder.

SUSPECTS

TOWNIE TAUPE

He can't technically vote in the election, but he can intimidate the opposition for you.

6'3" • LEFT-HANDED • BLUE EYES • BLOND HAIR

CANDIDATE RED

He has invented an entirely new system of canvassing, an entirely unexploited method of political persuasion: threats of physical violence.

6'2" • LEFT-HANDED • BROWN EYES • BROWN HAIR

CANDIDATE HONEY

He cares about what the other students care about. And not just because they told him what they care about first. Or because he wants to win the election. I mean, it's partially those things, but it's about more than that, too.

6'0" • LEFT-HANDED • HAZEL EYES • BROWN HAIR

TRAILBLAZER TANGERINE

You know, you can't be trailblazing all the time. Sometimes you just want to relax and enjoy yourself. And sometimes you want to set aside your own relaxation to join a movement. Or fight against one!

5'5" • LEFT-HANDED • HAZEL EYES • BLOND HAIR

LOCATIONS

THE OLD DORMS
INDOORS

These don't have air conditioning. So, they're practically barbaric.

THE NEW DORMS
INDOORS

Good news—when they built these dorms, they added a state-of-the-art feature: landlines!

THE ROOFTOP OVERLOOK
OUTDOORS

Here you can have a great view of the sidewalk. Why you would want a great view of a sidewalk is your own business.

THE SIDEWALK BETWEEN THEM
OUTDOORS

You can walk from the old dorms to the new dorms on this sidewalk. Wow! Amazing!

WEAPONS

A BEAUTIFUL TEXTURED JACKET
HEAVY-WEIGHT • MADE OF COTTON

It looks like it costs a fortune. But that's where you're wrong: it actually costs two fortunes.

A POLITICAL SIGN
MEDIUM-WEIGHT • MADE OF PAPER & WOOD

So people can hear what you're yelling about with their eyes.

A POLITICAL FLYER
LIGHT-WEIGHT • MADE OF PAPER

This is making arguments so infuriating it'll give you an aneurysm.

A HARPSICHORD
HEAVY-WEIGHT • MADE OF WOOD (MOSTLY)

They don't put harpsichords in school bands that often anymore. But back then, they all had one.

WHAT SHOES THEY WERE WEARING

 COMFORTABLE SNEAKERS

 SOME SWEET SANDALS

 FANCY-PANTS LOAFERS

 BIG, GIANT BOOTS

CLUES & EVIDENCE

- Candidate Honey was on the sidewalk between the two dorms.

- The second tallest suspect was carrying a political sign, which sort of made them the tallest suspect.

- Townie Taupe was trespassing in the new dorms.

- A beautiful textured jacket was discovered on the rooftop overlook.

- Trailblazer Tangerine was not wearing big, giant boots. Not their style.

- The person who was wearing comfortable sneakers was in the old dorms.

- A weapon containing paper was brought by the person who was wearing fancy-pants loafers.

- An infuriating argument was read outdoors.

- **A harpsichord was used to commit the murder.**

WEAPONS

LOCATIONS

SHOES

WHO?

WHAT?

WHERE?

AND?

23. SPEAKER FOR THE DEAD

Junior Logico attended the campaign speech of Candidate Honey, excited to support his friend as he was running for office. However, when he attended the speech, he found him preoccupied—not with the speech he was about to give, but with the murder that had just occurred: a supporter had died!

SUSPECTS

TRAILBLAZER TANGERINE

When your goal is to be the first nonbinary student to graduate Deduction College, you have two primary obstacles: graduating Deduction College, and *any other nonbinary student.*

5'5" • LEFT-HANDED • HAZEL EYES • BLOND HAIR

CANDIDATE HONEY

He seems really in his element surrounded by Honeybees (which is what his supporters have started to call themselves). He's making big promises, and he mostly seems to mean them.

6'0" • LEFT-HANDED • HAZEL EYES • BROWN HAIR

STRAIGHT-A CRIMSON

Her politics are still in development: Will she become a titan of the working class or a brilliant defender of the status quo? At an expensive college, either can happen!

5'9" • LEFT-HANDED • GREEN EYES • RED HAIR

THE MYSTERIOUS IRRATINO

Just because Logico knows his name doesn't make him any less mysterious. In fact, in many ways, he's more mysterious. What kind of name is Irratino anyway? *Ir-rah-tea-no . . .*

6'2" • LEFT-HANDED • EMERALD-GREEN EYES • GREAT BROWN HAIR

LOCATIONS

THE BIG STAGE
OUTDOORS

This is a hastily built stage that's certain to collapse at the worst possible moment. But maybe, if we're lucky, the funniest.

THE CROWD BELOW
OUTDOORS

Everybody is milling around, talking politics while they wait for the speech to begin.

THE STATUE OF GRAYSTONE
OUTDOORS

Logico has made progress decoding this statue. The first word is REMEMBER. Is this a cryptogram?

THE FOUNTAIN
OUTDOORS

Somebody fell into this and shouted "Eureka!" and it got a lot of laughs.

WEAPONS

A MEGAPHONE
MEDIUM-WEIGHT • MADE OF PLASTIC & TECH

You can use this to magnify your voice, or to minimize someone's lifespan.

A DICTIONARY
HEAVY-WEIGHT • MADE OF PAPER

It has the definition of every word ever spoken except one. Which?

THE SPEECH ITSELF
LIGHT-WEIGHT • MADE OF PAPER

A lot of it is about the importance of school spirit and rooting for the chessboxing team.

A LETTER OPENER
MEDIUM-WEIGHT • MADE OF METAL

Open a letter or a major artery.

WHAT MINDSET THEY'RE IN

 BORED OUT OF THEIR MIND

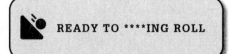 READY TO ****ING ROLL

 ANGRY! FURIOUS! INCONSOLABLE!

 OPEN-MINDED TO WHAT WILL BE SAID

CLUES & EVIDENCE

- The person with the speech itself was bored out of their mind.

- A brown hair (or maybe a great brown hair?) was found on the megaphone.

- Trailblazer Tangerine was ready to ****ing roll. But roll for whom? Or for what? And what does it mean to roll?

- The person who was open-minded to what would be said was on the big stage.

- A message was written in the Previous Letter Code: UIF QFSTPO XIP XBT SFBEZ UP ****JOH SPMM XBT OPU CZ UIF GPVOUBJO.

- Candidate Honey was seen in the crowd below.

- A letter opener was in the hands of the person who shouted "Eureka!"

- **A dictionary was found beside the former supporter.**

SUSPECTS   MINDSET   LOCATIONS

WEAPONS

LOCATIONS

MINDSET

WHO?

WHAT?

WHERE?

AND?

24. I HOPE YOU DON'T GET CUT (IN EITHER SENSE)

Meanwhile, Junior Logico did not think he was going to make the varsity chessboxing team. His chess was too aggressive and his boxing was too analytical. So he decided to train harder than anybody else. Unfortunately, everybody else decided to do that, too. Everybody except one: one was murdered.

SUSPECTS

ASSISTANT COACH RASPBERRY

He wants to have the best chessboxing team this school has ever seen, which is going to be hard, because for the last ten years, they've had some of the worst chessboxing teams the school has ever seen.

6'0" • LEFT-HANDED • BLUE EYES • BLOND HAIR

PRODIGY ROSE

He was a great chess prodigy as a child. But honestly, at this point, he's a little old to be calling himself a prodigy. But he's not yet a grandmaster.

5'7" • LEFT-HANDED • BROWN EYES • BROWN HAIR

NEW RECRUIT BLAZE

She is desperate to qualify for the varsity chessboxing team. If she doesn't, she doesn't know what she'll do. This is her life. This is all she cares about!

5'8" • RIGHT-HANDED • GREEN EYES • BLOND HAIR

HOT SHOT MAROON

He's a punk kid who thinks he's better than everyone else on the team. And, unfortunately, due to the immense sums of money expended on his early education, he's mostly right.

6'2" • RIGHT-HANDED • HAZEL EYES • RED HAIR

LOCATIONS

THE WEIGHT ROOM
INDOORS

It's wild that fundamentally one of the best exercises you can do is just picking up heavy things.

THE BIG LOOP
OUTDOORS

This is a loop around the school. Each student athlete is expected to do one hundred each semester.

THE CHESS LIBRARY
INDOORS

If you want to get good at chessboxing, you have to hit the books. Then, you have to study them.

THE OBSTACLE COURSE
OUTDOORS

A bunch of tires lined up that you've gotta jump through.

WEAPONS

AN ACTUAL HORSE
HEAVY-WEIGHT • MADE OF 100 PERCENT HORSE

Its beauty and majesty are most fully expressed when it's trampling someone.

A PENKNIFE
LIGHT-WEIGHT • MADE OF METAL

The penknife is mightier than the sword (and easier to sneak into a building, or a person).

THE CHAMPIONSHIP CHESS-BOXING TROPHY
HEAVY-WEIGHT • MADE OF METAL

Honestly, the older this trophy gets, the less proud people are, and the more embarrassed.

THE ROPES
MEDIUM-WEIGHT • MADE OF SWEET, SWEET VELVET

"He's on the ropes!" someone might say. That's better than the ropes being around your neck.

THEIR BIGGEST STRENGTH

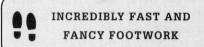 INCREDIBLY FAST AND FANCY FOOTWORK

 SOLID, DEPENDABLE POSITIONAL PLAY

 REEEALLY BOOKED UP ON THE OPENINGS

 WILLING TO RISK IT ALL EVERY TIME

CLUES & EVIDENCE

- Hot Shot Maroon brought a penknife.

- Prodigy Rose did not bring a weapon with beauty or majesty.

- The suspect who was willing to risk it all every time was seen outdoors.

- The person with an actual horse did not have incredibly fast and fancy footwork.

- Either Hot Shot Maroon or Prodigy Rose had solid, dependable positional play.

- The ropes were discovered on the big loop.

- Prodigy Rose was reeeally booked up on the openings.

- Green eyes were reflected off some weights in the weight room.

- **The murder took place in the chess library.**

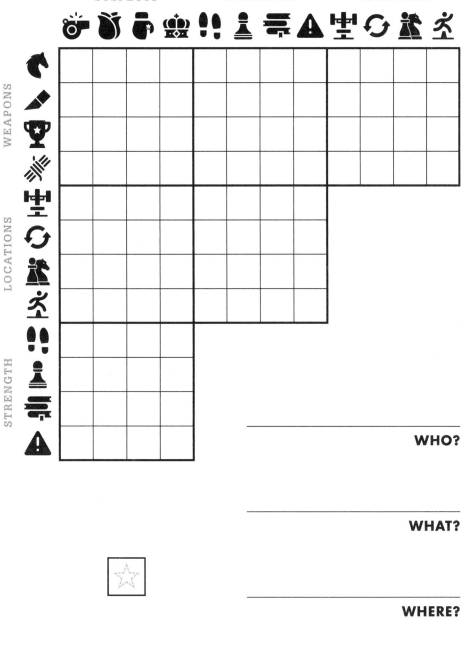

SUSPECTS   STRENGTH   LOCATIONS

WEAPONS

LOCATIONS

STRENGTH

WHO?

WHAT?

WHERE?

AND?

25. THE PRUNING OF THE ARBORETUM

To show what his candidacy could do for the school, Candidate Honey led his Honeybees into the arboretum, not to restore it to its original state, but to make it into a beautiful garden park. Unfortunately, it was proving difficult. Not only was it incredibly overgrown, but also, a worker had been killed.

SUSPECTS

AMBITIOUS MAUVE

She is determined to graduate Deduction College in three years, instead of the typical four, so that she can move on to her life's ambition (which is definitely not global domination through big-tech financial schemes).

5'8" • RIGHT-HANDED • BROWN EYES • BLACK HAIR

RICH KID CHAMPAGNE

He's volunteering to help clean up the arboretum. And hey, it kind of feels good to give back. (And then, after giving back, going to drink some very expensive wine.)

5'11" • LEFT-HANDED • HAZEL EYES • BLOND HAIR

BOTANIST ONYX

All the plants being destroyed. The nature, the wildlife. It haunts her. She can't believe what's become of the beautiful forest in the middle of campus. It's a loss from which she might never recover.

5'0" • RIGHT-HANDED • BROWN EYES • BLACK HAIR

CANDIDATE HONEY

He's doing a great job of directing the entire operation and telling everybody what to do. But, if you look closely, you'll see that he's not actually doing any work at all.

6'0" • LEFT-HANDED • HAZEL EYES • BROWN HAIR

LOCATIONS

THE FORMERLY MYSTERIOUS BUILDING
INDOORS

Okay, so, it turns out it was a bathroom.

THE NO-LONGER-HIDDEN POND
OUTDOORS

Now that all the weeds have been cut away, it needed a new name.

THE BEAUTIFUL GATE
OUTDOORS

When they cleaned off the moss, it turns out the letters didn't spell ENTER. They spelled DYSENTERY.

THE COBBLESTONE PATH
OUTDOORS

Replacing the dirt with cobblestones was one of the nicest (and most expensive) renovations.

WEAPONS

SOME COOL ROCKS
MEDIUM-WEIGHT • MADE OF ROCKS

You're not supposed to take anything from the arboretum, but cool rocks are hard to resist.

A CHAINSAW
HEAVY-WEIGHT • MADE OF METAL & TECH

One of the best tools for chopping down a tree or accidentally cutting your arm off.

A REGULAR OL' SAW
MEDIUM-WEIGHT • MADE OF METAL

Honestly, if you have this one, you're super jealous of the person with a chainsaw.

A LAWNMOWER
HEAVY-WEIGHT • MADE OF METAL & TECH

People get run over by lawnmowers all the time, especially if a murderer is driving.

WHAT THEY WANT TO DO IN THE PARK WHEN IT REOPENS

 THEATER. IMMERSIVE THEATER.

 FRACKING AND/OR CRYPTO-MINING

AN ANIMAL RESCUE & COFFEE SHOP

WHATEVER PEOPLE WANT THE MOST

CLUES & EVIDENCE

- The suspect who wanted to make the park an animal rescue & coffee shop was seen outdoors.

- The second tallest suspect had a medium-weight weapon.

- Whoever was by the beautiful gate had a heavy-weight weapon.

- The person by the no-longer-hidden pond had plans. Big plans. Immersive theater plans.

- The suspect who was carrying a regular ol' saw also had brown eyes.

- Whoever had a great tool for cutting your own arm off was left-handed (for now, at least).

- Ambitious Mauve thought this would be a great location for fracking and/or crypto-mining.

- Candidate Honey was seen on the III XV II II XII V XIX XX XV XIV V XVI I XX VIII. (See Exhibit A.)

- Botanist Onyx did not want to do whatever people wanted to do: she had her own plans.

- A regular ol' saw was not found by the no-longer-hidden pond.

- **The worker's body was found in the formerly mysterious building.**

SUSPECTS   PARK   LOCATIONS

WEAPONS

LOCATIONS

PARK

WHO?

WHAT?

WHERE?

AND?

26. THE DEBATE OF DEATH

It was finally debate day at Deduction College, and there were four candidates on stage, representing the four major student parties on campus. Unfortunately, the conversation degenerated into something of a ruckus, and by the time the debate was over, one of the security guards had been killed.

SUSPECTS

CANDIDATE RED

Candidate Red started his campaign by denouncing the corrupt practices of Deduction College and the craven collaboration of his fellow candidates. And since then, he's gone negative.

6'2" • LEFT-HANDED • BROWN EYES • BROWN HAIR

CANDIDATE HONEY

Honey has been telling the people exactly what they want to hear, and it turns out they love it, which is exactly what he wants to hear. So it's working out for everybody!

6'0" • LEFT-HANDED • HAZEL EYES • BROWN HAIR

CANDIDATE RULEAN

He keeps getting disqualified and expelled for murder, but he keeps showing up and insisting he hasn't been disqualified.

5'8" • RIGHT-HANDED • BLUE EYES • RED HAIR

MODERATOR GRAYSCALE

This student has promised he will never have an opinion on anything whatsoever, making him the perfect moderator.

5'6" • RIGHT-HANDED • BLUE EYES • BLOND HAIR

LOCATIONS

THE LEFT PODIUM
INDOORS

Just to get this out of the way first: we're measuring these from the audience's perspective.

THE CENTER PODIUM
INDOORS

This would be the center podium regardless of what the audience's perspective was.

THE RIGHT PODIUM
INDOORS

The person at this podium kept saying they were the right one to vote for . . . it got annoying.

THE MODERATOR TABLE
INDOORS

This person has the impossible task of leading a civilized conversation between people who want to kill each other.

WEAPONS

A GIANT PILE OF NOTECARDS
MEDIUM-WEIGHT • MADE OF PAPER

Notes for the debate, or a meticulous plan for murder?

A DICTIONARY
HEAVY-WEIGHT • MADE OF PAPER

This clearly shows that the candidates are standing behind "lecterns," not "podiums."

A MICROPHONE
MEDIUM-WEIGHT • MADE OF METAL

Just what you wanted: for politicians to be louder.

A FANCY WRISTWATCH
MEDIUM-WEIGHT • MADE OF METAL

This is the kind of watch you wear when a rich donor is funding your campaign.

THEIR MOST MEMORABLE LINE

 "I'LL PROMISE YOU ANYTHING YOU WANT, AND I'LL TRY TO DELIVER."

 "EVERYBODY, STOP THROWING THINGS AT EACH OTHER!"

 "IF WE DON'T WIN WITH VOTES, WE'LL WIN THROUGH OTHER MEANS."

 "MY NAME IS CANDIDATE HONEY, AND I WANT TO BE YOUR PRESIDENT."

CLUES & EVIDENCE

- First of all, just to get this out of the way, Moderator Grayscale was sitting at the moderator table.

- Candidate Red brought a dictionary.

- A fancy wristwatch was found at the center podium.

- The person who said, "If we don't win with votes, we'll win through other means," was not at the right podium.

- Hilariously, it was not Candidate Honey who said, "My name is Candidate Honey, and I want to be your president." It was Candidate Rulean, in what has to be one of the all-time biggest gaffes.

- The suspect with a giant pile of notecards also had blue eyes.

- A weapon made of metal was brought by the person who said, "Everybody, stop throwing things at each other!"

- A student journalist scribbled down Candidate Honey's most memorable line, but they wrote all the letters and words out of order: "DNA NATW OYU LIL EELRVID ESIRPOM ILL UYO YRT TO IANGHYNT."

- **A microphone was found beside the victim.**

WEAPONS

LOCATIONS

MEMORABLE LINE

WHO?

WHAT?

WHERE?

AND?

27. BEFORE THE MATCH, AFTER THE MURDER

Junior Logico was ecstatic! As a member of the varsity chessboxing team, he was going to get to compete in the regional chessboxing championship that was being held at Deduction College. However, before the match, his opponent was murdered. This meant it was an easy win for him, but it was a difficult case to crack!

SUSPECTS

ASSISTANT COACH RASPBERRY

Not many people know that the famous Coach Raspberry got his start teaching college chessboxing, but it's true.

6'0" • LEFT-HANDED • BLUE EYES • BLOND HAIR

CANDIDATE HONEY

A man of the people. He's for the people, by the people, of the people, just as long as the people support him.

6'0" • LEFT-HANDED • HAZEL EYES • BROWN HAIR

THE MYSTERIOUS IRRATINO

He acts like it's urgent to talk to Logico, but he won't explain why.

6'2" • LEFT-HANDED • EMERALD-GREEN EYES • GREAT BROWN HAIR

CHESSBOXER BLAZE

She's great at boxing because she loves punching faces, and she's great at chess because she loves killing kings.

5'8" • RIGHT-HANDED • GREEN EYES • BLOND HAIR

LOCATIONS

THE DUCTS
INDOORS

Nobody really appreciates the value of a good duct.

THE LOCKERS
INDOORS

Logico's locker is much neater than his teammates'. A note in it says, "The last word of the second section is LOGIC."

THE WASHROOMS
INDOORS

Where you wash off after a particularly grueling round of chess.

THE EQUIPMENT CLOSET
INDOORS

Nobody knows what all is in here but everybody knows it smells bad.

WEAPONS

A CHESS CLOCK
MEDIUM-WEIGHT • MADE OF WOOD & METAL

Maybe you're the one who gets clocked! Then you're really out of time.

THE HEAVY BAG
HEAVY-WEIGHT • MADE OF STUFFING & CANVAS

For practicing your punches, or flattening your adversaries.

A FRAMED PHOTOGRAPH
MEDIUM-WEIGHT • MADE OF WOOD, GLASS, & PAPER

Great to remind you of who you're fighting for.

A GIANT SWORD
HEAVY-WEIGHT • MADE OF METAL

Part of a chess knight cosplay taken too seriously: this replica weapon is actually sharp.

FAVORITE CHESSBOXING BOOK

 BY ROOK OR LEFT HOOK: HOW TO WIN AT CHESSBOXING

 KING OF THE RING: THE BIOGRAPHY OF A CHAMPION

 WHITE AND BLACK AND BLUE: A HISTORY OF CHESSBOXING

 THE BISHOP'S IN A BOX: A DAME OBSIDIAN MYSTERY

CLUES & EVIDENCE

- The suspect just as tall as Candidate Honey was not in the ducts.

- A framed photograph was found in the washrooms.

- The tallest suspect had a copy of *White and Black and Blue: A History of Chessboxing.*

- Whoever was hiding in the lockers was right-handed.

- The person with the heavy bag had been studying *By Rook or Left Hook: How to Win at Chessboxing.*

- The suspect with a giant sword was known to have hazel eyes.

- Chessboxer Blaze grew up reading *King of the Ring: The Biography of a Champion*, hoping that one day she would be the champion.

- **The body of Logico's opponent was found in the equipment closet.**

WEAPONS

LOCATIONS

CHESSBOXING BOOK

WHO?

WHAT?

WHERE?

AND?

28. THE STUDENT UNION OF LIFE AND DEATH

At the student union, the only topics of conversation were the upcoming election, the upcoming chessboxing national championship, and the murder of the janitor in the student union. Really, you'd think that would be a bigger issue, but everybody had kinda gotten used to all the murders.

SUSPECTS

WHIZ-KID NIGHT

Their superior mathematical faculties have allowed them to make some pretty advantageous wagers on the chessboxing match: by hedging their bets, they are guaranteed to make money, no matter who wins.

5'9" • LEFT-HANDED • BLUE EYES • BROWN HAIR

STRAIGHT-A CRIMSON

She has been studying nonstop, but are they medical textbooks or socialist theory?

5'9" • LEFT-HANDED • GREEN EYES • RED HAIR

CANDIDATE HONEY

He has announced that he is suspending his campaign in order to travel with the chessboxing team and cheer them on. "Our school winning is more important than me winning," he says.

6'0" • LEFT-HANDED • HAZEL EYES • BROWN HAIR

THE MYSTERIOUS IRRATINO

The Mysterious Irratino has been extra mysterious today. He's not really making eye contact with Logico. Is something suspicious going on? Can he be trusted?

6'2" • LEFT-HANDED • EMERALD-GREEN EYES • GREAT BROWN HAIR

LOCATIONS

THE PRESIDENT'S OFFICE
INDOORS

Well, the president of the students, at least.

THE HIGH BALCONY
OUTDOORS

It looks out over the whole campus. Definitely a picturesque place to die.

THE COURTYARD
OUTDOORS

There're a bunch of hedges here, but unfortunately not enough to make a maze.

THE FOOD COURT
INDOORS

If this was a real court, the cooks would be tried for crimes against humanity.

WEAPONS

A POISONED APPLE
MEDIUM-WEIGHT • MADE OF APPLE & TOXINS

If you're a teacher and you get an apple, ask yourself if the student wants you dead.

A TRUMPET
MEDIUM-WEIGHT • MADE OF METAL

Half of the freshmen are given a roommate who plays the trumpet. (The other half are given a trumpet.)

A RUBY PIN
LIGHT-WEIGHT • MADE OF METAL & A GEMSTONE

These pins are everywhere. There has to be some connection between them. But what?

AN IVORY SCEPTER
HEAVY-WEIGHT • MADE OF IVORY

This plays an important part in the graduation ceremonies. It's worth its weight in ivory.

WHO THEY THINK WILL WIN THE CHESSBOXING TOURNAMENT

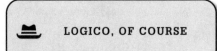 LOGICO, OF COURSE

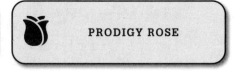 PRODIGY ROSE

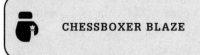 CHESSBOXER BLAZE

 CHAMPION GOLD

CLUES & EVIDENCE

- Candidate Honey was obviously, 100 percent completely and fully behind Logico, of course!

- Straight-A Crimson did not think that Prodigy Rose would win: he was lacking in the boxing part of chessboxing.

- A ruby pin was discovered in the president's office.

- Whoever was at the food court had a medium-weight weapon.

- The person with a ruby pin did not think that Logico would win. Impossible.

- Someone with a medium-weight weapon thought Chessboxer Blaze would win.

- The person with an ivory scepter was confident that Champion Gold would win.

- The Mysterious Irratino was seen with a poisoned apple.

- A trumpet was discovered in the courtyard.

- **The janitor's body was found on the high balcony.**

SUSPECTS   TOURNAMENT   LOCATIONS

WHO?

WHAT?

WHERE?

AND?

29. THE BEGINNING OF THE ENDGAME

Logico could not believe that he had made it all the way to the national college chessboxing championship. But now, there could only be one winner! Who would it be? Chessboxer Blaze, Champion Gold, Prodigy Rose, or Junior Logico? Finally, a mystery that doesn't involve someone being murdered. What a relief!

COMPETITORS

JUNIOR LOGICO

He's been training his entire time at Deduction College for this, and he really wants to do a good job. Plus, Candidate Honey is really cheering him on from the crowd. He's completely giving up the election to support him!

6'0" • RIGHT-HANDED • BROWN EYES • BLACK HAIR

CHESSBOXER BLAZE

Probably the only equally balanced chessboxer in the world. Her father was a world-champion boxer, and her mother was the greatest chess player of her generation. (When they got together, you can imagine the articles that were written!)

5'8" • RIGHT-HANDED • GREEN EYES • BLOND HAIR

CHAMPION GOLD

Look, just because you're the World Chessboxing Champion and you murder someone at one college (see Case 6: The Opening Position of the Body) doesn't mean you can't be recruited by another college to win a college tournament for their school.

6'2" • RIGHT-HANDED • BROWN EYES • BROWN HAIR

PRODIGY ROSE

He's the greatest chess player on the team, that's for sure. But here's the secret of chessboxing: being really good at chess doesn't always correlate to being really good at boxing, too. In fact, if you had to say, it probably correlates to you being worse.

5'7" • LEFT-HANDED • BROWN EYES • BROWN HAIR

LOCATIONS

THE ROPES
INDOORS

You can lean against these ropes as part of a divisive strategy, or just because you're tired.

THE CORNER
INDOORS

Where your coach tells you to ignore reason in favor of believing that you've got this!

OUT OF THE RING
INDOORS

Generally, if you're knocked out of the ring, that's considered a bad thing.

THE DEAD CENTER
INDOORS

This is where they set up the chessboard between boxing rounds.

WEAPONS

A SOLID RIGHT HOOK
LIGHT-WEIGHT • MADE OF HANDS

It's wild to be staring straight at someone and then he punches you from the left.

12
THE OL' ONE-TWO
LIGHT-WEIGHT • MADE OF HANDS

You hit them with the one, and then, when they think that's all you've got—WHAM!—the two.

AN INESCAPABLE CHECKMATE
LIGHT-WEIGHT • MADE OF HANDS

You could stare at this position for hours, you'll never find a way out.

A WILD HAYMAKER
LIGHT-WEIGHT • MADE OF HANDS

This is one of the hardest punches to land or to get hit by.

TO WHOM THEY WOULD DEDICATE THEIR VICTORY

 TO THE MANY MURDER VICTIMS

 TO EVERYONE WHO EVER DOUBTED THEM

 TO THEMSELVES (AND THEIR OWN GLORY)

 TO DEDUCTION COLLEGE

CLUES & EVIDENCE

- Chessboxer Blaze won her match with a solid right hook.

- The shortest suspect was seen hanging around on the ropes.

- The person who would dedicate their victory to Deduction College was out of the ring.

- The person who won with an inescapable checkmate would dedicate their victory to themselves (and their own glory).

- Champion Gold was suspicious of the person who used the ol' one-two.

- Junior Logico was shocked by the other suspect who won his match with the ol' one-two.

- The person who won their game with an inescapable checkmate was not in the dead center of the ring.

- Whoever would dedicate it to the many murder victims was right-handed.

- Junior Logico was seen hanging around in the dead center of the ring.

- **The chessboxing national champion won by a wild haymaker.**

| | COMPETITORS | | | | VICTORY | | | | LOCATIONS | | | |

WEAPONS

LOCATIONS

VICTORY

WHO?

WHAT?

WHERE?

AND?

30. ELECTION DAY TO DIE

After Logico won the chessboxing championship, he traveled with Candidate Honey to his after party, where they would also celebrate Honey's almost certainly successful campaign. Logico was happy to support his friend, but he was also beginning to piece together a series of facts. Someone had engineered Logico's victory. But who?

SUSPECTS

THE MYSTERIOUS IRRATINO

Logico can't let his personal relationships get in the way of accurately ascertaining just who the heck is responsible for these crimes.

6'2" • LEFT-HANDED • EMERALD-GREEN EYES • GREAT BROWN HAIR

CHESSBOXER BLAZE

She's great at boxing because she loves punching faces, and she's great at chess because she loves killing kings.

5'8" • RIGHT-HANDED • GREEN EYES • BLOND HAIR

CANDIDATE HONEY

A man of the people. He's for the people, by the people, of the people, just as long as the people support him.

6'0" • LEFT-HANDED • HAZEL EYES • BROWN HAIR

CANDIDATE RED

In the final stretch of campaigning, when the polls started to show him losing, he began to argue that the electoral process was not how you made true political change.

6'2" • LEFT-HANDED • BROWN EYES • BROWN HAIR

LOCATIONS

THE CHESSBOXING GYM
INDOORS

The pride and joy of the school. Also, maybe, something they take a little too seriously.

THE STUDENT UNION
INDOORS

The center of student power, which—in the ultimate scheme of things—means nothing.

THE GREEK THEATRE
INDOORS

The plays are written and performed in English. So how come people keep calling it Greek?

THE GARDEN PARK
OUTDOORS

This is already overrun with vines and weeds. Calling it a garden park is just a straight-up lie.

AN IMPORTANT OBJECT

THE FIRST OBJECT

This is from ten years ago, and it makes people depressed now. (See Case 21: The Dead Can't Vote (Or Can They?).)

THE SECOND OBJECT

This keeps you warm and it's in two colors—black and white. (See Case 16: The Stayover Slaying.)

THE THIRD OBJECT

An object you'd have to be really smart to use to kill. (See Case 15: The Mid-Game Murder.)

THE FOURTH OBJECT

This is all about school spirit and the importance of rooting for the chessboxing team. (See Case 23: Speaker for the Dead.)

MOTIVES

 TO WIN AN ELECTION

 TO GET SWEET, SWEET REVENGE

 FOR BLOODY REVOLUTION

 AS AN ACCIDENT DURING A MATCH

CLUES & EVIDENCE

- The suspect who would kill for bloody revolution had a weapon made at least partially of paper.

- Everybody knew that Candidate Honey wanted to win the election. And honestly, everybody also knew that he would kill for it.

- The person in the building connected to the dining hall would only kill as an accident during a match. (See Exhibit A.)

- The Mysterious Irratino was waving a weapon that seemed too tiny to kill.

- Whoever had a knitted weapon was right-handed.

- Whoever was in the garden park had a light-weight weapon.

- The suspect who was at the Greek Theatre had brown eyes.

- **The entire operation was organized out of the chessboxing gym.**

SUSPECTS MOTIVES LOCATIONS

IMPORTANT OBJECT

LOCATIONS

MOTIVES

_____ **WHO?**

_____ **WHAT?**

_____ **WHERE?**

_____ **WHY?**

SENIOR

> To beguile the time, look like the time.
>
> —Lady Macbeth, *Macbeth*

Finally, senior year! Senior Logico walked across the campus quad, looking up at the buildings that had become so well known to him. And yet somehow, the more he knew about Deduction College, the more it remained a mystery to him.

What were the ruby pins he had seen all throughout campus?

Who were the robed figures that Logico had seen wandering campus at night?

And what was the real story behind the death of Lord Graystone, the founder of the school, who had died in mysterious—and some might say impossible—circumstances?

These were idle curiosities, of course, until the effigy of Dean Tuscany was found hanging in front of the student union with the message THE COLLEGE DIES THIS YEAR taped to a shoe with red tape. That didn't seem like a positive sign.

Obviously, this was something Logico was going to have to investigate. He felt like a degree from a defunct institution was going to be worth a lot less on the job market.

But this section features some of the most difficult challenges because, for the first time, Logico is going to interview the suspects and hear their statements. He'll have to put all of his logical abilities to the test, because this will always be true: the murderer will always lie, and the other suspects will always tell the truth.

To solve these puzzles, you'll have to see what it would mean for each suspect to be lying. Check each suspect: Can you logically complete the deduction grid when you assume they are lying and everyone else is telling the truth? If so, then they are the murderer. But if you reach a contradiction—like two suspects having a single weapon, or nobody being at a specific location—then you know they are innocent, and it must be someone else.

If these puzzles are still too easy for you, then for extra credit see if you can identify the original founder of the secret society that's been running around campus for years, and who is running it now.

Perhaps it's obvious to you. Perhaps Logico is blind to what is right in front of him.

A MAP OF THE TUNNELS BENEATH CAMPUS

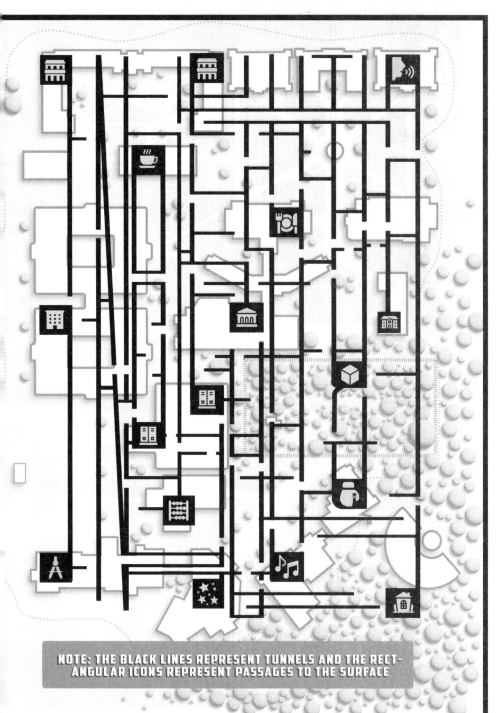

NOTE: THE BLACK LINES REPRESENT TUNNELS AND THE RECT-
ANGULAR ICONS REPRESENT PASSAGES TO THE SURFACE

31. THE TRAGIC FATE OF LORD GRAYSTONE

One of the most famous legends at the school is never told on the tours, because it's just too dark. But the truth is, the founder of the school, Lord Graystone himself, was killed after the college had been open for only a few years. The crime is almost as famous as its perpetrator!

SUSPECTS

EARL GREY

A long line of Earl Greys is descended from this Earl Grey. And the tea had yet to be named after him. At that point, he was famous mostly for being a feudal lord.

5'9" • RIGHT-HANDED • BROWN EYES • WHITE HAIR • CAPRICORN

FIRST STUDENT EMINENCE

This fresh-faced young man was there when the school opened.

5'2" • LEFT-HANDED • GRAY EYES • BROWN HAIR • PISCES

OLD ROSY GARNET

He was the cofounder of the school with Lord Graystone in many people's eyes, though they were on opposite sides of almost every issue.

6'2" • RIGHT-HANDED • GRAY EYES • GRAY HAIR • GEMINI

LOCATIONS

A BIG OL' FIELD
OUTDOORS

They're thinking of planting one or two trees here. It's such a beautiful open space.

A CUBE UNDER CONSTRUCTION
OUTDOORS

Supposedly an alum is paying for this. But the wild thing is, nobody has graduated yet . . .

NEW MAIN
INDOORS

They just recently built this building. It looks great, brand new, and it'll never look bad!

WEAPONS

A BEJEWELED DAGGER
MEDIUM-WEIGHT

Look, this is the kind of weapon that someone uses to betray a close friend.

A SCHOOL CHARTER
LIGHT-WEIGHT

An official document that declares that the school should teach logic alone.

A TABLET
MEDIUM-WEIGHT

Back then, you wrote on a little tiny chalkboard you held in your hand called a "tablet."

CLUES & EVIDENCE

* A Gemini was in New Main, and that fact, for some reason, was deeply important.

* Earl Grey brought a school charter.

STATEMENTS & DIARY ENTRIES

(Remember: The murderer is lying. The others are telling the truth.)

Earl Grey: First Student Eminence was walking in the field.

First Student Eminence: Sirs, Earl Grey was examining a cube under construction.

Old Rosy Garnet: The bejeweled dagger was in the big field.

SUSPECTS   LOCATIONS

WEAPONS

LOCATIONS

WHO?

WHAT?

WHERE?

32. GONE IN THE DARK OF THE NIGHT

In the middle of the first night of Logico's senior year, a visiting alumnus vanished on campus. According to the CCTV cameras, only three suspects were on campus during the time of the crime. One of them was responsible. But how did they do it? Logico was determined to find out.

SUSPECTS

FULL DEAN TUSCANY

Now they've been promoted to full dean, and they're allowed to sit on the Council of Deans. It's a phenomenal rise for an assistant professor.

5'5" • LEFT-HANDED • GREEN EYES • GRAY HAIR • LIBRA

BOTANIST ONYX

She knows the genus and species of every single plant in the world, and at Deduction College, that actually makes you pretty cool.

5'0" • RIGHT-HANDED • BROWN EYES • BLACK HAIR • VIRGO

THE MYSTERIOUS IRRATINO

Now that Logico knows his name, this year we'll learn what his whole deal is.

6'2" • LEFT-HANDED • EMERALD-GREEN EYES • GREAT BROWN HAIR • AQUARIUS

LOCATIONS

THE ASTRONOMY BUILDING
INDOORS

Here you can study the only stars bigger than the ones in Hollywood.

THE ABANDONED BUILDING
INDOORS

Once, like all abandoned buildings, it was the newest building on the block.

RHETORIC HALL
INDOORS

Don't say you don't like this building or you'll have to listen to a speech about why you're wrong.

WEAPONS

A LEATHER-BOUND DISSERTATION
HEAVY-WEIGHT

It's killed two already: the cow for the leather, and its first reader by boredom.

A BOTTLE OF A PROHIBITED BEVERAGE
MEDIUM-WEIGHT

This isn't allowed on campus (unless you're really, really cool).

A COMMEMORA-TIVE PEN
LIGHT-WEIGHT

It says "Deduction College: Where Truth Lives," but someone has scratched out the V.

CLUES & EVIDENCE

- The Mysterious Irratino stayed away from abandoned buildings for three reasons: common sense, divine revelation, and a past experience.

- A Libra was at the location with a tunnel entrance that connected to the tunnel entrance in the student union. (See Exhibits A & D.)

STATEMENTS

(Remember: The murderer is lying. The others are telling the truth.)

Full Dean Tuscany: Botanist Onyx did not bring a prohibited beverage.

Botanist Onyx: If I tell you, can I get back to my work? Irratino brought a bottle of a prohibited beverage.

The Mysterious Irratino: A commemorative pen was not in Rhetoric Hall.

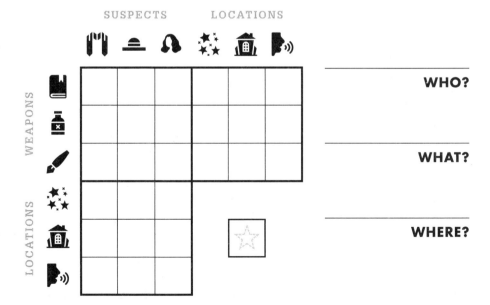

33. THE MYSTERY OF THE ABANDONED BUILDING

Originally built to house the humanities department, this building has long been abandoned. As Logico crept through the cobweb-lined hallways, he thought about all the things he'd rather be doing. But then, he tripped over a body wearing robes and another one of those blasted ruby pins!

SUSPECTS

JOHNNY BLUESKY

He is being his regular American college student self, doing regular American college student things like investigating abandoned buildings, which all American college students do.

6'2" • LEFT-HANDED • BROWN EYES • BLACK HAIR • ARIES

FOODIE AUBERGINE

She's famous around campus for having a very elevated sense of taste. What's she doing in an abandoned building? She's, uh, well, she's . . . looking for rare mushrooms? Right, yes.

5'2" • RIGHT-HANDED • BLUE EYES • BLOND HAIR • LIBRA

RA COPPER

Currently, she's a resident advisor. And she's making sure that nobody is breaking any of the rules on campus. And the most important of those rules is to do whatever RA Copper says.

5'5" • RIGHT-HANDED • BLUE EYES • BLOND HAIR • ARIES

LOCATIONS

THE COBWEBBED CLASSROOM
INDOORS

Old desks sit covered in cobwebs. In many ways, it's become a classroom for arachnids.

THE CREEPY BASEMENT
INDOORS

The steps are dangerous. But most dangerous is what awaits you at the bottom!

THE RICKETY ROOFTOP
OUTDOORS

There's probably no place on campus that's more dangerous, just from an accident perspective.

WEAPONS

A TINY BEAN-STUFFED ANIMAL
LIGHT-WEIGHT • MADE OF COTTON & BEANS

Economists are predicting this collectible might outperform the S&P 500.

A WOODEN BATON
MEDIUM-WEIGHT • MADE OF WOOD

Supposedly way less lethal than a metal baton, but if you tried hard enough . . .

A HEAVY BLACK ROBE
HEAVY-WEIGHT • MADE OF WOOL

This robe is heavy, black, and covered in cat hair.

CLUES & EVIDENCE

- The suspect who was carrying a highly performing financial asset had brown eyes.

- Foodie Aubergine had not been in the creepy basement.

STATEMENTS

(Remember: The murderer is lying. The others are telling the truth.)

Johnny Bluesky: Based on my readings of Marx . . . Twain: a heavy black robe was on the rickety rooftop.

Foodie Aubergine: RA Copper was holding a wooden baton.

RA Copper: I was in the cobwebbed classroom.

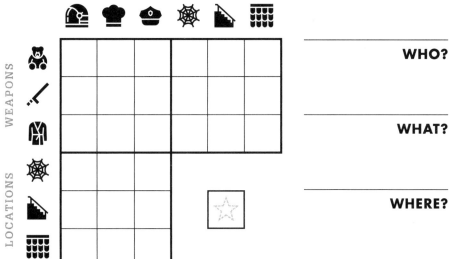

34. THE SHADOWS OF THE MANSION

The Mysterious Irratino took Logico on a long walk, then said, "We're here." They were standing in front of a mansion that made the chancellor's mansion look like a hovel, and Logico could not believe it when Irratino simply walked in the front door. This was Irratino's house! Another shock came when they discovered Irratino's dead butler: Who has a butler?

SUSPECTS

SKEPTIC SEASHELL

He doesn't believe in anything at all except not believing in anything, which he believes in fully. He was visiting for his weekly argument with Irratino.

5'7" • RIGHT-HANDED • GREEN EYES • GRAY HAIR • PISCES

WHIZ-KID NIGHT

They were able to calculate that there were forty-six different explanations that all made more sense than them being the murderer.

5'9" • LEFT-HANDED • BLUE EYES • BROWN HAIR • PISCES

THE GREAT HEIR IRRATINO

Holy moly, Irratino is loaded! Logico couldn't believe this place. Having a butler die in a mysterious way seemed way more plausible than having a mansion. That was the real mystery!

6'2" • LEFT-HANDED • EMERALD- GREEN EYES • GREAT BROWN HAIR • AQUARIUS

LOCATIONS

THE GRAND FIREPLACE
INDOORS

Imagine a classic fireplace. That's what this is. It's in a cavernous hall.

THE GRAND DECK
OUTDOORS

This is the kind of patio that you could rent out for events, like a coronation or a state funeral.

THE GRAND BEDROOM
INDOORS

Logico has never seen a larger bed, except maybe at the bottom of a river.

WEAPONS

A SHIP IN A BOTTLE
MEDIUM-WEIGHT • MADE OF GLASS & WOOD

How did they get this ship inside that bottle? And was it just used to kill someone?

A FAMILY PORTRAIT
HEAVY-WEIGHT • MADE OF OIL, CANVAS, & WOOD

An oil painting of the Great Heir Irratino with his two moms. They seem happy.

A VELVET-UPHOLSTERED CHAIR
HEAVY-WEIGHT • MADE OF VELVET & WOOD

Made from delicate wood and upholstered with fine velvet.

CLUES & EVIDENCE

- An Aquarius was on the grand deck.

- Skeptic Seashell did not bring a ship in a bottle: it was too big to get through the door.

STATEMENTS

(Remember: The murderer is lying. The others are telling the truth.)

Skeptic Seashell: According to my theories, Whiz-Kid Night brought a family portrait.

Whiz-Kid Night: Based on the numbers, I was beside the grand fireplace.

The Great Heir Irratino: A velvet-upholstered chair was in the grand bedroom.

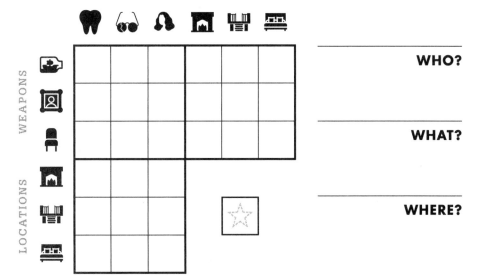

35. THE TRAGEDY OF THE IRRATINOS

Irratino's parents had been on a research expedition to Amaranth Island when a horrible accident claimed both their lives. Or, at least, that was the story. But when Logico looked through the papers, which included some old newspaper accounts of the tragedy, there seemed to be more to the story than met the eye . . .

SUSPECTS

SEA CAPTAIN SALT

He's the most trustworthy captain in the sea, he is, at least according to him, that is.

5'8" • RIGHT-HANDED • BLUE EYES • GRAY HAIR • CANCER

IRRATINO'S MOTHER

This is the mom from whom Irratino gets his irrepressible love of the crystals, candles, astrology, and everything else esoteric.

5'0" • RIGHT-HANDED • GREEN EYES • RED HAIR • AQUARIUS

IRRATINO'S OTHER MOTHER

And this is the mom from whom Irratino gets his more far-out opinions.

5'9" • LEFT-HANDED • BROWN EYES • BLACK HAIR • PISCES

LOCATIONS

AMARANTH ISLAND
OUTDOORS

A rocky island with a mysterious woods but absolutely no lighthouse.

THE OPEN OCEAN
OUTDOORS

It's just ocean as far as you look in any direction.

A SHIP AT SEA
INDOORS

This ship seems a lot older than Logico would have guessed.

WEAPONS

A SILVER LOCKET
LIGHT-WEIGHT • MADE OF
METAL & PAPER

This belonged to
one of Irratino's
moms and the
picture inside is of
his other one.

A RUBY KEY
LIGHT-WEIGHT • MADE OF
METAL & A GEMSTONE

Well, most of the
key is silver. But
it has a big ruby
in it!

A SIGNET RING
LIGHT-WEIGHT • MADE OF
METAL

A signet ring was
like the ID of the
past. Or maybe
like the pass-
word? Or maybe
the signature?

CLUES & EVIDENCE

- Sea Captain Salt sailed back alone on the ship.

- Years later, the silver locket was found on Amaranth Island.

STATEMENTS FROM DIARY ENTRIES

(Remember: The murderer is lying. The others are telling the truth.)

Sea Captain Salt: Argh! The ruby key fell into the open ocean.
Irratino's Mother: My wife had the silver locket.
Irratino's Other Mother: I was stranded on Amaranth Island.

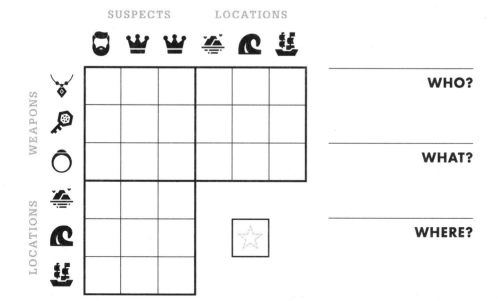

36. DEATH BENEATH THE STARS

The next night was the annual astronomy field trip, and Logico was excited to go because he knew he would see Irratino there, and he had just decoded his letter. He thought he'd found the perfect moment to tell him, in the middle of a lunar eclipse, but then they heard a scream: a fellow stargazer had been murdered.

SUSPECTS

JOHNNY BLUESKY

A wholesome, all-American kid. Nobody knows that he's secretly a Soviet spy. Well, that's what he thinks, at least. The Russian accent is actually pretty thick.

6'2" • LEFT-HANDED • BROWN EYES • BLACK HAIR • ARIES

ASTRONOMER SLATE

Everyone wants to take the astronomy class from Slate, the youngest astronomy professor the school has ever had.

5'5" • LEFT-HANDED • BROWN EYES • BROWN HAIR • AQUARIUS

THE GREAT HEIR IRRATINO

Now that Logico knows Irratino's story, he looks at him a lot differently. Like, for example, he looks at how great his hair is.

6'2" • LEFT-HANDED • EMERALD-GREEN EYES • GREAT BROWN HAIR • AQUARIUS

LOCATIONS

THE GRASSY KNOLL
OUTDOORS

Nothing bad ever happened on a beautiful grassy knoll.

A PARKED CAR
INDOORS

A great place to make out, but also, the trunk could fit two or three bodies.

THE SHADY TREE
OUTDOORS

At night it's more like a star-blocking tree, isn't it?

WEAPONS

A MOON ROCK
MEDIUM-WEIGHT

Actually, it would be more gram-matically correct to say the moon rocks.

A BOOK OF STAR NAMES
HEAVY-WEIGHT

Every star has a name, like "that bright one" or "that one over there."

A TELESCOPE
HEAVY-WEIGHT

A tool to make things that are far away seem near— like the end of your life!

CLUES & EVIDENCE

- A moon rock was certainly not on the grassy knoll.

- An Aries was in a XVI I XVIII XI V IV III I XVIII. (See Exhibit A.)

STATEMENTS

(Remember: The murderer is lying. The others are telling the truth.)

Johnny Bluesky: Based on the eternal science of Marxism-Leninism: Astronomer Slate brought a book of star names.

Astronomer Slate: A telescope was under the shady tree.

The Great Heir Irratino: I brought a telescope.

SUSPECTS   LOCATIONS

WEAPONS

LOCATIONS

WHO?

WHAT?

WHERE?

37. A DEATH IN THE PARK AFTER DARK

The Great Heir Irratino led Senior Logico to Disgraced Honey's garden park. Without his political manipulations, plans had begun to reclaim the park. Logico didn't know where Irratino was leading him. He also didn't know who was responsible for the body they had just found in the park.

SUSPECTS

WHIZ-KID NIGHT

They swear that the only reason they were in the park was to calculate the rate at which the weeds are growing, but Logico wasn't sure if "watching the grass grow" was a plausible activity.

5'9" • LEFT-HANDED • BLUE EYES • BROWN HAIR • PISCES

TOWNIE TAUPE

People keep asking him to leave campus (on account of he's a murderer), but he makes the very good point that a lot of people are doing a lot of murdering and it's unfair to single him out.

6'3" • LEFT-HANDED • BLUE EYES • BLOND HAIR • TAURUS

PET PERSON CLOUD

They have more pets than you could possibly imagine. They have deadly spiders, toxic fish, and—most dangerous of all—two rabbits.

5'7" • RIGHT-HANDED • GRAY EYES • BLOND HAIR • SCORPIO

LOCATIONS

THE WEEDY PATH

OUTDOORS

Logico remembers this being cobblestones only a year ago.

THE GIANT CEMENT CUBE

OUTDOORS

Nobody knows what it's for. Or even what it is. But the vines are starting to reclaim it.

THE NEWISH GATE

OUTDOORS

This gate was new a year ago, but it's already starting to rust again.

WEAPONS

A MOTORIZED RAKE
HEAVY-WEIGHT • MADE OF METAL & TECH

If you can put a motor on a saw, why not on a rake?

A KILLER SNAKE
MEDIUM-WEIGHT • MADE OF SNAKESKIN, ETC.

The difficult part is training the snake to be sneaky.

A POP QUIZ
LIGHT-WEIGHT • MADE OF PAPER

This has a bunch of trivia questions about the Deduction College. (See Appendix D.)

CLUES & EVIDENCE

• Townie Taupe was briefly chased by the person who brought a killer snake.

• The suspect at the big stone cube was a Scorpio.

STATEMENTS

(Remember: The murderer is lying. The others are telling the truth.)

Whiz-Kid Night: I was not by the newish gate.

Townie Taupe: A motorized rake was not on the weedy path.

Pet Person Cloud: A killer snake was on the weedy path.

SUSPECTS   LOCATIONS

WEAPONS

LOCATIONS

WHO?

WHAT?

WHERE?

38. TERROR IN THE TOMB OF INTUITION

"Welcome to the Tomb of Intuition, our headquarters," said the Great Heir Irratino, as he led Logico down the stone steps into darkness. As he followed, Logico began to realize how little he really knew about this Irratino, and how, nevertheless, he still trusted him . . . at least until they stumbled over another body.

SUSPECTS

BOTANIST ONYX

She has begun to tell people that her plants are speaking to her, and everybody is a little worried that she doesn't mean it metaphorically. But what if she's telling the truth?

5'0" • RIGHT-HANDED • BROWN EYES • BLACK HAIR • VIRGO

"PHILOSOPHER" BONE

Okay, so maybe a better name for this kid is Pretentious Bone, but he showed up to school and immediately introduced himself as a philosopher.

5'1" • RIGHT-HANDED • BROWN EYES • BALDING • TAURUS

THE GREAT HEIR IRRATINO

What are the things that Logico actually even knows about this guy? Maybe he doesn't even live in that mansion, maybe his parents aren't dead, maybe they sell insurance in Des Moines.

6'2" • LEFT-HANDED • EMERALD-GREEN EYES • GREAT BROWN HAIR • AQUARIUS

LOCATIONS

THE STONE BUST
INDOORS

The stone face of this bust has been smashed. What are they trying to hide?

THE GIANT PORTRAIT
INDOORS

The face has been ripped off of this portrait of the secret society's founder. Who does it depict?

THE SARCOPHAGUS
INDOORS

Latin for "super-creepy coffin." A plaque says that the founder himself is buried inside.

WEAPONS

A SECRET HANDSHAKE
MEDIUM-WEIGHT • MADE OF THOUGHTS, REALLY

The secret of this handshake is that it kills the person you do it with.

A RUBY KEY
LIGHT-WEIGHT • MADE OF METAL & A GEMSTONE

This was the key that let them in, but did it show somebody else out?

A POUCH OF MAGICK POWDERS
LIGHT-WEIGHT • MADE OF CANVAS & POWDER

What is "magick" about these powders is that they are deadly.

CLUES & EVIDENCE

- Clearly, as we've established, Irratino had the ruby key.

- Someone who talks to plants was by a smashed stone face.

STATEMENTS (IN HIGH LATIN)

(Remember: The murderer is lying. The others are telling the truth.)

Botanist Onyx: Phusilusosusophuserum Busoneum wusasum nusotum busyum thuseum susarcusophusagusum.

"Philosopher" Bone: Aum wuseapusonum musaduseum ofum thusoughtsum wusasum busyum thuseum susarcusophusagusum.

The Great Heir Irratino: Susomeusoneum wusasum ususingum aum susecrusetum husandusshusakeum busyum thuseum stusoneum busustum.

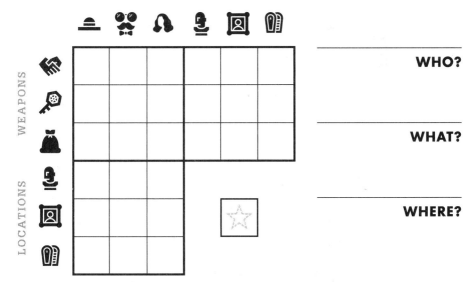

39. THE MYSTERIES OF THE UNIVERSE

The Great Heir Irratino led Logico down a dark tunnel to a giant door. And again, Irratino used the ruby key and the door opened, and on the other side . . . "Behold the mysteries of the universe!" Irratino declared. But Logico wanted to know if the dead body was one of those mysteries.

SUSPECTS

WHIZ-KID NIGHT

They've been at the scene of so many murders that, at this point, it would be truly irrational to suspect them. Have they not proved that they were innocent so many times before?

5'9" • LEFT-HANDED • BLUE EYES • BROWN HAIR • PISCES

THE GREAT HEIR IRRATINO

He had been leading Logico down into the darkness, so surely his movements were accounted for, right? Not really, because in the darkness, they had become separated briefly.

6'2" • LEFT-HANDED • EMERALD-GREEN EYES • GREAT BROWN HAIR • AQUARIUS

SOCIOLOGIST UMBER

As a representative from the hard sciences, Sociologist Umber is always asking people to question their priors and if they've read Weber.

5'4" • LEFT-HANDED • BLUE EYES • BLOND HAIR • LEO

LOCATIONS

THE COLLECTION OF MYSTERY
INDOORS

Three exhibits—real objects that don't seem possible—are usually stored here.

THE PARADOXICAL LIBRARY
INDOORS

They have every book here that isn't collected in any other library.

THE RITUAL ROOM
INDOORS

This is a room for rituals. But what kind of rituals? Hopefully, nice ones . . .

WEAPONS

A STRANGE FORK
MEDIUM-WEIGHT • MADE
OF MINDF***

This fork seems
to be one thing on
one side and an-
other on the other.

A BIZARRE CUBE
MEDIUM-WEIGHT • MADE
OF CONTRADICTIONS

The cube seems
to exist in many
dimensions, visi-
ble in this world
only as a shadow.

**AN IMPOSSIBLE
TRIANGLE**
MEDIUM-WEIGHT • MADE
OF THE INEFFABLE

This triangle
turns in on itself.
It hurts Logico's
head to look at it.

CLUES & EVIDENCE

- The suspect in the collection of mystery had blond hair.

- The tallest suspect did not bring a bizarre cube.

STATEMENTS (IN HIGH LATIN)
(Remember: The murderer is lying. The others are telling the truth.)

Whiz-Kid Night: Susociusolusogistum Umusbuserum brusoughtum
aum strusangeum fusorkum.

The Great Heir Irratino: A strusangeum fusorkum wusasum inum
thuseum rusitusualum rusoomum.

Sociologist Umber: Whusizum-Kusidum Nusightum brusoughtum anum
impusossusibluseum trusiangusleum.

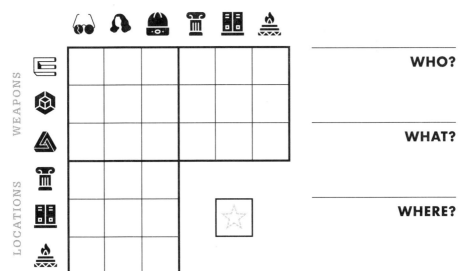

40. THE GRADUATION TO END ALL GRADUATIONS

Full Dean Tuscany stood up at graduation, but instead of giving a typical speech about the value of education, she announced that a secret society had been uncovered that was plotting against the school. Then, she presented her evidence to the graduates.

SUSPECTS

WHIZ-KID NIGHT

They insist that the murder that Logico witnessed was just a dream. But wait, how did they know what Logico dreamt?

5'9" • LEFT-HANDED • BLUE EYES • BROWN HAIR • PISCES

FULL DEAN TUSCANY

As a teacher, she was beloved. As a dean, she is feared. Her quiet ascent from the bottom of the status pile to the near top is something every aspiring academic should study.

5'5" • LEFT-HANDED • GREEN EYES • GRAY HAIR • LIBRA

THE GREAT HEIR IRRATINO

He was watching from the audience as Dean Tuscany gave one of the most intense graduation speeches he had ever heard.

6'2" • LEFT-HANDED • EMERALD-GREEN EYES • GREAT BROWN HAIR • AQUARIUS

TOWNIE TAUPE

He won't stay off campus, despite the repeated requests, followed by the legal demand, followed by the attempt to physically restrain him.

6'3" • LEFT-HANDED • BLUE EYES • BLOND HAIR • TAURUS

WHAT CLUBS THEY LEAD

THE INTUITIVE INQUISITION
SUPER SECRET

A pretty unsettling name for a secret society, honestly. The Inquisition? I don't know, man . . .

THE COUNCIL OF DEANS
NOT SECRET

Going back to the beginning of the school, the Council of Deans is the one consistency on campus.

THE TEA SOCIETY
INVITATION ONLY

This is a club for only the most refined and dignified.

123

THE COUNTING CLUB
DESPERATE FOR MEMBERS

Okay, so it might not be as badass as the tea club, but it still counts.

HOW YOU SHOW YOUR LEADERSHIP

A RUBY DAGGER
LIGHT-WEIGHT—MADE OF METAL & A GEMSTONE

This is the famous dagger from the story about the death of Lord Graystone.

A COMMEMORATIVE MUG
MEDIUM-WEIGHT—MADE OF CERAMIC

There's a fifty-fifty shot that it arrives in the mail broken, or that you smash it over someone's head.

THE IVORY SCEPTER
HEAVY-WEIGHT—MADE OF IVORY

Finally, the big day to actually use the famous ivory scepter.

A COMPASS
LIGHT-WEIGHT—MADE OF METAL

Not the kind you use to find things, the kind you use to draw things. (Or stab people.)

FOUNDER

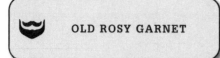 OLD ROSY GARNET

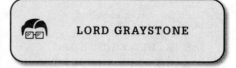 LORD GRAYSTONE

 EARL GREY

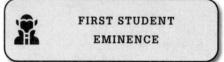 FIRST STUDENT EMINENCE

CLUES & EVIDENCE

- The Council of Deans was founded by Lord Graystone.

- This might surprise you, but Townie Taupe was actually the leader of the Tea Club.

- The ruby dagger actually did not contain a ruby (just like the ruby pins). No, they used a gemstone that shared its name with the founder of that club.

- Whiz-Kid Night was the leader of a club founded by First Student Eminence.

- Townie Taupe was not in a club founded by Old Rosy Garnet, that old devil.

- Irratino was a leader of a group mentioned in the letter he gave Logico. (See Appendix C.)

STATEMENTS

(Remember: The murderer is lying. The others are telling the truth.)

Whiz-Kid Night: Of course I am the leader of the Counting Club.

Full Dean Tuscany: I had the ivory scepter, fair and square.

The Great Heir Irratino: No, I didn't have the ruby dagger.

Townie Taupe: I don't have a compass, or even know what one is.

LEADERSHIP

CLUBS

FOUNDER

WHO?

WHAT?

HOW?

WHO FOUNDED?

Study Abroad

Doubt thou, the stars are fire,

Doubt that the sun doth move,

Doubt truth to be a liar,

But never doubt I love.

—*Hamlet*, act 2, scene 2

After graduation, Deductive Logico had expected to be thrilled to go out into the world, applying the means of deductive reasoning to solve all the world's problems. Instead, he was depressed, because he had followed the rules of logic and it had led him to heartbreak.

When he felt honored by Chancellor Oak, he had discovered that he was a fraud, and he had to expose him. When he felt challenged by Dame Obsidian, he had been forced to reveal her secret scheme. When he joined the chessboxing team, and was excited to vote for Candidate Honey, he had realized both were a scam.

And finally, when he met someone who made his heart leap with joy, someone he wanted to share his deductions with, solve mysteries with, and argue with forever, he had learned—only too late—that the Great Heir Irratino was just like the others.

So instead of going out into the world, he decided to stay behind and work on a doctoral dissertation on the value of logic and how you must pursue logical deductions no matter where they lead: not looking away from the conclusions you draw, no matter how difficult they may be for you to accept.

Fortunately, the newly named Chancellor Tuscany offered Logico funding to travel the world and research his dissertation, which was tentatively titled "Logical Deduction and its Discontents." However, he was also asked to do a small amount of work in each place that he visited, meeting with old alumni and requesting donations for the school.

Logico did this, but at night, he would look up at the stars and wonder if Irratino was looking at the same stars and seeing the same constellations. Was there anything worth turning your back on logic?

In these ten cases, you'll be tested on everything you've learned from Deduction College. Not only will you have to figure out the motives in each case, but you'll have to discover which suspect is lying, as well.

For extra credit, follow Logico's gut and look for clues that might exonerate Irratino, point the finger at someone else, and reveal the true secrets of Deduction College, which could change everything Logico thinks he knows about logic, mystery, and murder. It was irrational to believe such evidence existed, and yet, as Logico looks up at the stars, a part of him still believes.

A DIAGRAM OF THE STARS ABOVE

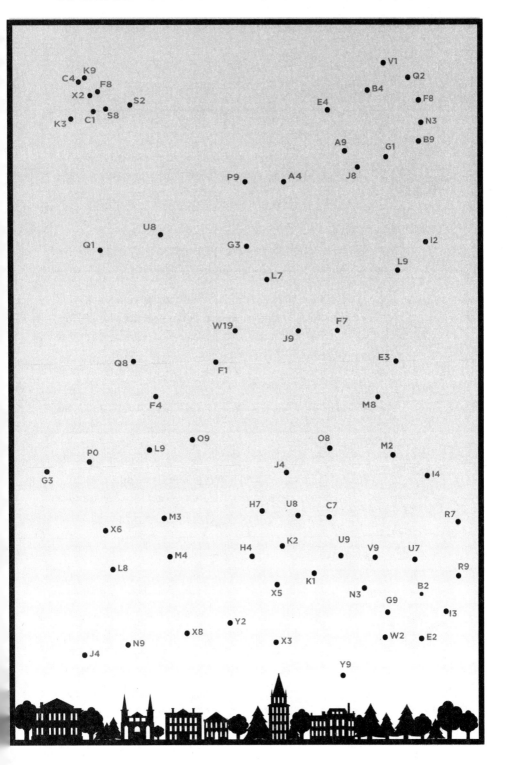

41. MURDER AROUND THE WORLD

With funding from Deduction College the now Deductive Logico traveled around the world, gathering materials for his doctoral thesis, but also soliciting donations from alumni. Combining these two goals would have been more than enough work, but he also had to solve the murder of the person who had this job before him.

SUSPECTS

VISCOUNT EMINENCE

The oldest man you have ever met. He outlived his children and was born before his father.

5'2" • LEFT-HANDED • GRAY EYES • BROWN HAIR • PISCES

VICE PRESIDENT MAUVE

She is the vice president of TekCo Futures, a company that promises to change the world. How they'll actually do that remains a closely guarded secret.

5'8" • RIGHT-HANDED • BROWN EYES • BLACK HAIR • TAURUS

COSMONAUT BLUSKI

He has finally revealed himself as a spy, and he was disappointed that everybody already knew.

6'2" • LEFT-HANDED • BROWN EYES • BLACK HAIR • ARIES

CHANCELLOR TUSCANY

One of the biggest success stories in modern academia, Tuscany went from an assistant professor to chancellor in four years. She keeps a red tape dispenser on her desk to remind her what she needs to cut through to get things done.

5'5" • LEFT-HANDED • GREEN EYES • GRAY HAIR • LIBRA

LOCATIONS

HOLLYWOOD
OUTDOORS

Tinseltown, the City of Angels, La La Land, the Dream Factory.

DEDUCTION COLLEGE
OUTDOORS

The school where Logico has spent his last four years. In a way, he'll never leave.

NEW AEGIS
OUTDOORS

A town for hippies, UFO enthusiasts, and (inevitably) scammers.

THE REPUBLIC OF DRAKONIA
OUTDOORS

Once this was the Holy Republic of Drakonia. Now, it's run by Major Red.

WEAPONS

A GOLDEN BIRD
HEAVY-WEIGHT • MADE OF GOLD

This flamingo statue is worth a fortune.

A RED HERRING
MEDIUM-WEIGHT • MADE OF FISH

If you hold it by the tail, you can get some real momentum behind it.

A BOOBY-TRAPPED FEDORA
MEDIUM-WEIGHT • MADE OF [REDACTED]

Whatever you do, don't try it on.

A HEAVY CODEBOOK
HEAVY-WEIGHT • MADE OF PAPER

Filled with keywords and ciphers, you can use it to crack codes or skulls.

MOTIVES

 TO MAINTAIN THEIR POWER

 TO HELP WITH THEIR CAREER

 TO PROTECT THEIR SECRET IDENTITY

 TO STOP A REVOLUTION

CLUES & EVIDENCE

- The second shortest suspect brought a golden bird.

- Vice President Mauve was seen hanging around in New Aegis.

- Viscount Eminence was seen hanging around in a country run by Major Red.

- The person who might kill to help with their career was not in Hollywood.

- Forensics determined a weapon made at least partially out of paper was present at Deduction College.

- A weapon made in part of paper was brought by the person who wanted to protect their secret identity.

- The person with a booby-trapped fedora wanted to stop a revolution.

STATEMENTS

(Remember: The murderer is lying. The others are telling the truth.)

Viscount Eminence: I was not at Deduction College.

Vice President Mauve: Viscount Eminence might kill to help with his career . . .

Cosmonaut Bluski: Viscount Eminence was not in New Aegis.

Chancellor Tuscany: As the holder of six PhDs, let me just say: whoever had the booby-trapped fedora wanted to stop a revolution.

WEAPONS

LOCATIONS

MOTIVES

WHO?

WHAT?

WHERE?

WHY?

42. MURDER IN THE MOUNTAINS

In the Screaming Forest of Drakonia, Deductive Logico met with Alumnus Red, who was now going by the title Major Red, and honestly, it suited him well. He wouldn't make a donation to Deduction College (which he called capitalist indoctrination), but he did ask Logico to help solve the murder of his lieutenant.

SUSPECTS

RADICAL CRIMSON

She got straight As in Deduction College, but somehow her fierce intelligence has not managed to get her control over Major Red's guerilla army. If she were running things, the Iron Tsar would be dead by now.

5'7" • LEFT-HANDED • GREEN EYES • RED HAIR • LIBRA

MAJOR RED

One of the biggest lessons he learned in Deduction College is not to bother with elections but to just take power by force. But one of the downsides of his new method is that it involves a lot more sleeping in the woods.

6'2" • LEFT-HANDED • BROWN EYES • BROWN HAIR • ARIES

COMRADE CHAMPAGNE

Sure, capitalism is bad, but honestly, living in the mountains, waging a guerilla war against the Drakonian government, that doesn't suit him. He needs to be at a soirée somewhere.

5'11" • LEFT-HANDED • HAZEL EYES • BLOND HAIR • CAPRICORN

MILITANT LEAD

Whatever the ultimate military aims are, Militant Lead is excited to pursue them. You tell him, "Once more into the breach." He asks, "Why only once?"

6'2" • RIGHT-HANDED • BROWN EYES • BLACK HAIR • VIRGO

LOCATIONS

THE BIG TENT
INDOORS

This tent is big enough to sleep like fifteen guerilla soldiers or one gorilla soldier.

A WEIRD-LOOKING ROCK
OUTDOORS

Some of the soldiers seem to think that this rock looks like it's making a rude gesture.

THE BOOBY TRAP
OUTDOORS

They dug a hole, put spikes in the bottom, and covered it with leaves. Then, they shot anybody who got close to it.

A TWISTED AND MANGLED TREE
OUTDOORS

This is a great way to mark where to make camp: "Set it up by that spooky tree!"

WEAPONS

THE TINY RED BOOKLET
LIGHT-WEIGHT • MADE OF PAPER

Filled with Major Red's one-liners, like, "The only thing worse than sucker-punching someone is being sucker-punched by someone else."

A GARLAND OF GARLIC
MEDIUM-WEIGHT • MADE OF VEGETABLE MATTER

This can keep Drakonian night eaters from your home and, if wrapped tightly around your neck, blood from your brain.

A SILVER BULLET
LIGHT-WEIGHT • MADE OF METAL

The Reds started a rumor that Major Red could only be killed by a silver bullet, and it was a great way to destroy the finances of the opposition.

A STICK OF CHEAP DYNAMITE
LIGHT-WEIGHT • MADE OF EXPLOSIVES

These would become famous all over the world as "Red bananas," a symbol of the Red Revolution's merciless power to overwhelm the old state.

MOTIVES

 TO INSTILL FEAR IN HIS TROOPS

 TO PUSH THE MAJOR LEFTWARD

 TO CREATE A PRETEXT FOR GOING HOME

 BECAUSE HE WAS FOLLOWING ORDERS

CLUES & EVIDENCE

- The person who would kill if he was ordered to do it was beside a natural feature that looked like it was making a rude gesture.

- In the booby trap, Logico saw a piece of silver.

- Radical Crimson wanted to push the army leftward. Not just politically, but also as a way to flank the forces of the Iron Tsar.

- The suspect with the Tiny Red Booklet also had brown hair.

- The person who wanted to create a pretext for going home had a weapon that resembled the constellation formed by these stars: S8 S2 U8 Q1 K3 C1 X2 C4 K9 F8 S8. (See Exhibit E.)

- Whoever wanted to instill fear in his troops was left-handed.

- Militant Lead had never been in the place that could sleep a gorilla.

STATEMENTS

(Remember: The murderer is lying. The others are telling the truth.)

Radical Crimson: Comrade Champagne was carrying a Red banana.

Major Red: By the revolution, I was just following orders.

Comrade Champagne: I must confess to you: whoever wanted to create a pretext for going home was in the big tent.

Militant Lead: Major Red did not bring a garland of garlic.

SUSPECTS MOTIVES LOCATIONS

WEAPONS

LOCATIONS

MOTIVES

WHO?

WHAT?

WHERE?

WHY?

43. ONE MURDER, UNDER GOD

Next, Deductive Logico went to visit the Hillside Monastery. There, Alumni Brownstone, Mango, and Lapis had taken vows. They wouldn't donate, either (on account of their vows of poverty), but they requested he investigate the murder of one of their members, the previous head of the monastery.

SUSPECTS

SISTER LAPIS

At first, she missed her sisterhood in college. But now, she's found a sisterhood that she'll be able to stay in forever (and ever . . . and ever . . . and ever).

5'2" • RIGHT-HANDED • BROWN EYES • BROWN HAIR • CANCER

BISHOP AZURE

A bishop who has been visiting the monastery to check on the new recruits, and to ask them how her daughter had done in Deduction College.

5'4" • RIGHT-HANDED • BROWN EYES • BROWN HAIR • GEMINI

FATHER MANGO

If you had told him when he was in college that he could join the priesthood and keep drinking, he would have done it years ago. What's not to like? Free food, free lodging, and free wine!

5'10" • LEFT-HANDED • BROWN EYES • BALD • TAURUS

BROTHER BROWNSTONE

He is a devout man of God who wants to put his partying days behind him. But just when he thinks he's out, they'll pull him right back in . . .

5'4" • LEFT-HANDED • BROWN EYES • BROWN HAIR • CAPRICORN

LOCATIONS

THE CHAPEL
INDOORS

They've added some up-tempo numbers to the usual hymn rotation.

THE FORBIDDEN LIBRARY
INDOORS

Where they store the books the members aren't allowed to read.

THE CLIFFS
OUTDOORS

A great place to go to get closer to God because you're almost guaranteed to slip, fall, and die.

THE COURTYARD
OUTDOORS

A great place to sit and relax. Or to murder someone! Your choice.

WEAPONS

A HEAVY CANDLE
HEAVY-WEIGHT • MADE OF WAX

It's heavy, yet it lightens the room. A divine paradox, says Brother Brownstone.

SACRAMENTAL WINE
MEDIUM-WEIGHT • MADE OF GLASS & WINE

It's great branding for the church to associate God with wine. No notes.

A HOLY RELIC
MEDIUM-WEIGHT • MADE OF BONE

It's a totem of some long-forgotten god with a terrifying visage.

A POISONED GOBLET
HEAVY-WEIGHT • MADE OF METAL & TOXINS

It's filled with one of the greatest poisons known to mankind: alcohol.

MOTIVES

 AS PART OF A PARTY GONE WRONG

 TO MAINTAIN THEIR LEADERSHIP ROLE

 BECAUSE A VOICE TOLD THEM TO

 IN ORDER TO LEAVE THE MONASTERY

CLUES & EVIDENCE

- Bishop Azure had a totem of a long-forgotten god.

- Father Mango had a heavy-weight weapon.

- The person with a weapon exemplifying great branding might kill because a voice told them to.

- Sister Lapis was seen enjoying a beautiful place to sit and relax.

- The person who could kill as part of a party gone wrong was not in the forbidden library.

- Whoever was on the cliffs had a medium-weight weapon.

- Brother Brownstone was seen with what he called a "divine paradox."

STATEMENTS

(Remember: The murderer is lying. The others are telling the truth.)

Sister Lapis: Listen, whoever had the poisoned goblet wanted to maintain their leadership role.

Bishop Azure: Whoever wanted to leave the monastery was in the forbidden library.

Father Mango: Sister Lapis did not bring a heavy candle.

Brother Brownstone: I was certainly not in the chapel. Amen.

WEAPONS

LOCATIONS

MOTIVES

WHO?

WHAT?

WHERE?

WHY?

44. A CLASSIC DAME OBSIDIAN WHODUNIT

Deductive Logico was excited to visit his favorite former teacher, Dame Obsidian, even if she had turned out to be a murderer. Regardless, her lawyers had managed to keep her out of jail, and she welcomed Logico into her mansion with open arms and a small request: to solve the murder of her former writing assistant—former because he had just been brutally slain.

SUSPECTS

DAME OBSIDIAN

Now, she's written dozens more books and killed dozens more people, at least if the books are to be believed. (She does claim they're fiction, but she also includes a lot of wink emojis?)

5'4" • LEFT-HANDED • GREEN EYES • BLACK HAIR • LEO

BOOKIE-NOMINEE GAINSBORO

He's got a nomination for the Bookies coming up, and he's campaigning really hard for it. (Mostly by going incredibly negative against the other nominees.)

6'0" • LEFT-HANDED • HAZEL EYES • BROWN HAIR • GEMINI

EDITOR IVORY

Once she figured out that the world needed more sexy books, she started making money. Once she started making money, she started taking over.

5'6" • LEFT-HANDED • BROWN EYES • GRAY HAIR • SCORPIO

CHAIRMAN CHALK

Now, he runs the biggest bookstore in the world, and he publishes the biggest books in the world, and he rides on the biggest yacht in the world. All because textbooks and lattes are overpriced.

5'9" • RIGHT-HANDED • BLUE EYES • WHITE HAIR • SAGITTARIUS

LOCATIONS

THE GROUNDS
OUTDOORS

This beautifully maintained, completely unused yard is a true sign of wealth.

THE SPOOKY ATTIC
INDOORS

There's a legend that anybody who sleeps here will die before dawn. But that's silly; it's only happened twice—hardly legendary.

THE GREAT HALL
INDOORS

Every single Dame Obsidian novel in every single language over the last few years.

THE MASTER BEDROOM
INDOORS

If anyone else tries to sleep in Dame Obsidian's bed, there's a good chance they won't wake up.

WEAPONS

A FORK
LIGHT-WEIGHT • MADE OF METAL

As made famous in Dame Obsidian's bestselling novel *The Case of the Fork*.

AN AXE
MEDIUM-WEIGHT • MADE OF WOOD & METAL

This axe could chop a tree down. Or a person down!

A BOOBY-TRAPPED FEDORA
MEDIUM-WEIGHT • MADE OF [REDACTED]

She got criticized for this. People said it was outlandish. Well, they're not saying anything now.

VIAL OF POISON
LIGHT-WEIGHT • MADE OF GLASS & POISON

So many people have been poisoned in her books, it would be an honor to be killed like that.

MOTIVES

 TO WRITE A BESTSELLER

 TO CONQUER PUBLISHING FOREVER

 TO MAKE A MILLION DOLLARS

 TO CREATE ART (LOL, JK—FOR REVENGE)

CLUES & EVIDENCE

- Logico noticed that the person with the fork was using it with their dominant right hand.

- The person who wanted to write a bestseller had a weapon that resembled the constellation made from these stars: E4 B4 V1 Q2 F8 N3 B9 G1 I2 L9 A9 J8 E4. (See Exhibit E.)

- The person who wanted to make a million dollars was in the master bedroom.

- Editor Ivory was seen with a booby-trapped fedora.

- The suspect who wanted to conquer publishing forever had a weapon made at least partially of metal.

- Chairman Chalk had never been in the great hall.

- Bookie-Nominee Gainsboro was found indoors.

STATEMENTS

(Remember: The murderer is lying. The others are telling the truth.)

Dame Obsidian: A thought: Bookie-Nominee Gainsboro was in the great hall.

Bookie-Nominee Gainsboro: When I win the Bookie, you'll see that I brought a vial of poison.

Editor Ivory: Well, Dame Obsidian wanted to write a bestseller.

Chairman Chalk: Bookie-Nominee Gainsboro was not in the master bedroom.

SUSPECTS   MOTIVES   LOCATIONS

WEAPONS

LOCATIONS

MOTIVES

WHO?

WHAT?

WHERE?

WHY?

45. THE BEGINNING OF THE INSTITUTE

Deductive Logico visited a manor house in a small village that was undergoing some serious remodeling to turn it into "an institute for the investigation of things uninvestigable." That sure sounded familiar, and when he arrived, he understood immediately: Irratino greeted him at the door. "I want to talk to you, Logico," he said. "But first, we have a mystery I need you to solve."

SUSPECTS

MX. TANGERINE

They did it. They accomplished their goals. They did everything they wanted, and then some. Now what? Murder? Maybe.

5'5" • LEFT-HANDED • HAZEL EYES • BLOND HAIR • PISCES

INSPECTOR IRRATINO

Now, he's going by the title "inspector," and he's moved into the new headquarters of the Investigation Institute. He says that he was put under house arrest, so he moved to a bigger house.

6'2" • LEFT-HANDED • EMERALD- GREEN EYES • GREAT BROWN HAIR • AQUARIUS

OFFICER COPPER

She has been sent here to keep an eye on Inspector Irratino as he awaits his conspiracy trial. But hey, at least she gets to enjoy this unbelievable estate now.

5'5" • RIGHT-HANDED • BLUE EYES • BLOND HAIR • ARIES

NUMEROLOGIST NIGHT

They can explain not only the value of *x*, but the *meaning* of *x*. And they'll do it for anyone who listens for as long as they'll listen. (And then some.)

5'9" • LEFT-HANDED • BLUE EYES • BROWN HAIR • PISCES

LOCATIONS

THE GRAND CHATEAU
INDOORS

Built more than two hundred years ago and home to more than two hundred ghosts (they say).

AN IMPOSSIBLE HEDGE MAZE
OUTDOORS

People walk into it and never walk out. They send people to find them and it happens again.

THE BIG GATE
OUTDOORS

It has an ominous, foreboding quality to it that drives down the real estate prices.

THE GREAT TOWER
INDOORS

From here, you can see for miles. It's a great watchtower. But who needs a watchtower?

WEAPONS

A HYPNOTIC POCKET WATCH
LIGHT-WEIGHT • MADE OF METAL

If you look deeply into this watch, you can tell the time.

A CRYSTAL SKULL
MEDIUM-WEIGHT • MADE OF CRYSTAL

Maybe an actual alien's skull, or maybe just a fun art project.

A SELENITE WAND
MEDIUM-WEIGHT • MADE OF CRYSTAL

For casting spells and bashing skulls.

A POISONED CANDLE
MEDIUM-WEIGHT • MADE OF WAX

If you light this candle, everyone in the room will die. But it smells like lavender!

MOTIVES

 BECAUSE THEY WERE GETTING BORED

 TO PERCEIVE A GLIMPSE OF THE OVERALL

 TO UNDERSTAND THE COSMOS

 TO STEAL A REALLY EXPENSIVE ARTIFACT

CLUES & EVIDENCE

- Mx. Tangerine had a tool for casting spells and bashing skulls.

- The person who wanted to perceive a glimpse of the overall had a weapon that resembled the constellation made from these three sets of stars: C7 U9 K1 K2 U8 C7, G9 N3 V9 U7 B2 G9, and Y9 X3 X5 H4 H7 J4 O8 M2 I4 R7 R9 I3 E2 W2 Y9. (See Exhibit E.)

- Right-handed fingerprints were found on the big gate. Clearly, a right-handed person had passed through.

- Inspector Irratino smelled like lavender.

- The person who wanted to steal a really expensive artifact was in the (alleged) home of two hundred ghosts.

STATEMENTS

(Remember: The murderer is lying. The others are telling the truth.)

Mx. Tangerine: Whoever wanted to perceive a glimpse of the overall was in the great tower.

Inspector Irratino: Whoever had the poisoned candle wanted to understand the cosmos.

Officer Copper: Fine, I'll tell you: a selenite wand was in the great tower.

Numerologist Night: Whoever had the selenite wand wanted to steal a really expensive artifact.

SUSPECTS   MOTIVES   LOCATIONS

WEAPONS

LOCATIONS

MOTIVES

WHO?

WHAT?

WHERE?

WHY?

46. LIGHTS! CAMERA! MURDER!

Logico thought Midnight Studios looked like a place that might actually be able to make a donation to the school. It was huge, for one. And also everybody kept telling Logico how much money they made. But they weren't interested in donating to higher education. They were interested in the murder of an extra. Union rules required the crime be solved before filming could continue.

SUSPECTS

HACK BLAXTON

Unfortunately, it turns out that being very talented doesn't lead to half the success that being a complete and total hack does. He's made his choice, and he has no regrets.

6'0" • RIGHT-HANDED • BROWN EYES • BALD • SAGITTARIUS

MIDNIGHT III

He's the grandson of the founder of Midnight Studios, and he's just started work at the studio. He's going to be a big deal one day because he has big ideas. One in particular . . .

5'8" • LEFT-HANDED • BROWN EYES • BROWN HAIR • LIBRA

IT-GIRL ABALONE

She's the hottest new star in Hollywood and the paparazzi are following her everywhere, which is a real hassle because she's still shy. One day, maybe she'll kill somebody over it.

5'6" • RIGHT-HANDED • HAZEL EYES • RED HAIR • LIBRA

DIRECTOR DUSTY

Okay, so he said he wasn't going to sell out. But then he learned that, when you sell out, they pay you. So, uh, that was a revelation.

5'10" • LEFT-HANDED • HAZEL EYES • BALD • PISCES

LOCATIONS

MIDNIGHT STUDIOS
INDOORS

The biggest and most profitable studio in Hollywood . . . fifty years ago. Now they need something new. They're looking for a big movie. Or even a TV show!

THE FREEWAY
OUTDOORS

You can't get anywhere in Hollywood without going on the freeway. And you can't get anywhere on the freeway, either.

THE HOLLYWOOD SIGN
OUTDOORS

This is a giant sign that tells you where you are, in case you forget.

THE MAGIC PALACE
INDOORS

Hollywood's best magician-focused night club. (Also, the only one.)

WEAPONS

A CURSED SCREENPLAY
HEAVY-WEIGHT • MADE OF PAPER

So, half of Hollywood thought this script was cursed but it turns out the ink was just poisoned.

A DVD BOX SET
MEDIUM-WEIGHT • MADE OF WOOD

This is a luxurious box set meant to be an heirloom.

A "PROP" KNIFE
LIGHT-WEIGHT • MADE OF METAL & A THIN COATING OF RUBBER

Weirdly it's as sharp as a real knife.

AN AWARD
MEDIUM-WEIGHT • MADE OF METAL

This is the most prestigious award in Hollywood. Anybody would kill to get one.

MOTIVES

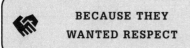 BECAUSE THEY WANTED RESPECT

 TO SAVE CINEMA

 JUST BEING WILD AND FAMOUS IN LA

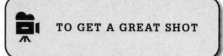 TO GET A GREAT SHOT

CLUES & EVIDENCE

- The person with a DVD box set did not want to be wild and famous in LA.

- Logico saw this constellation close to the ground, and he knew it was a vision of where the shortest suspect had been: M4 L8 N9 J4 G3 P0 X6 M3 L9 O9 Y2 X8 M4. (See Exhibit E.)

- Midnight III was seen hanging around in the Magic Palace.

- The suspect with the award also had no hair.

- The person who wanted respect was at Midnight Studios.

- Hack Blaxton had a medium-weight weapon.

- Whoever wanted to save cinema was left-handed.

STATEMENTS

(Remember: The murderer is lying. The others are telling the truth.)

Hack Blaxton: Picture it: whoever had the award wanted to save cinema.

Midnight III: Let me jump in: a cursed screenplay was on the freeway.

It-Girl Abalone: An award was not on the freeway.

Director Dusty: I'm very busy, but whoever wanted to get a great shot was on the freeway.

SUSPECTS   MOTIVES   LOCATIONS

WEAPONS

LOCATIONS

MOTIVES

WHO?

WHAT?

WHERE?

WHY?

47. THE CHESSBOXING WORLD CHAMPIONSHIP

Nowhere are you better able to study logic and its opposition than at the chessboxing world championship. Logico was embarrassed to find some people who recognized him for being the college chessboxing champion, even though he declined the honor. But he was proud of the fact that, when the referee was murdered, they all turned to him for help.

SUSPECTS

COACH RASPBERRY

Now, he coaches football, and he wins. But he's returned to support his former student as she makes her attempt at the grand prize.

6'0" • LEFT-HANDED • BLUE EYES • BLOND HAIR • ARIES

PRO CHESSBOXER BLAZE

She's great at boxing because she loves punching faces, and she's great at chess because she loves killing kings.

5'8" • RIGHT-HANDED • GREEN EYES • BLOND HAIR • LEO

HAS-BEEN GOLD

Some people call him Tarnished Gold, despite how often he reminds them that gold actually doesn't tarnish. But his glory days are definitely overshadowed by his gory days.

6'2" • RIGHT-HANDED • BROWN EYES • BROWN HAIR • LEO

GRANDMASTER ROSE

He finally made grandmaster, and he says he realized that repeatedly getting punched in the head was probably not great for his chess game. (But really, he just never spent the time drilling.)

5'7" • LEFT-HANDED • BROWN EYES • BROWN HAIR • SCORPIO

LOCATIONS

THE STANDS
INDOORS

Fans are cheering, "Take the knight!" or "Knock his head off!"

THE RING
INDOORS

This is where the million-dollar prize is going to be decided, by hook or by rook.

THE ROOFTOP LOUNGE
OUTDOORS

Where the rich hang out and bet on the blood/brainsport.

RINGSIDE
INDOORS

Here they've got a table set up with commentators: one knows chess, the other knows boxing.

WEAPONS

A CHESS BOOK
MEDIUM-WEIGHT • MADE OF PAPER

Who would buy a book that's just filled with puzzles and inscrutable diagrams?

A FOLDING CHAIR
HEAVY-WEIGHT • MADE OF METAL

Sometimes chessboxing gets out of hand, and somebody comes in with a folding chair . . .

BOXING GLOVES
MEDIUM-WEIGHT • MADE OF VINYL

Counterintuitive to use as a weapon, because they'll actually make your punches weaker.

A MYSTERIOUS PACKAGE
MEDIUM-WEIGHT • MADE OF ???

What's inside this mysterious package, and is it relevant to the plot?

MOTIVES

 TO PROVE THEIR OWN SUPERIORITY

 TO BE THE WORLD CHAMPION

 TO DESTROY THE COMPETITION

 TO BE REMEMBERED FOREVER

CLUES & EVIDENCE

- Whoever wanted to be the world champion was right-handed.

- Pro Chessboxer Blaze was seen hanging around next to someone chanting about a knight.

- Coach Raspberry wanted—as always—to destroy the competition.

- The suspect in the ring had blond hair.

- The person with a chess book wanted to prove their own superiority.

- The person who wanted to be remembered forever was ringside.

STATEMENTS

(Remember: The murderer is lying. The others are telling the truth.)

Coach Raspberry: Has-Been Gold brought a folding chair.

Pro Chessboxer Blaze: Whoever had the folding chair wanted to be remembered forever.

Has-Been Gold: Coach Raspberry did not bring a mysterious package.

Grandmaster Rose: Boxing gloves were ringside.

SUSPECTS   MOTIVES   LOCATIONS

WEAPONS

LOCATIONS

MOTIVES

WHO?

WHAT?

WHERE?

WHY?

48. THE MURDERER ON TRIAL FOR MURDER

Deductive Logico attended Ex-Chancellor Oak's trial, and he was shocked to realize that a lot of these murderers were getting more than expelled. "I promise," Chancellor Oak testified under oath, "that I never did anything except logically, and in the name of logic." Then the lights went off, and there was a scream. And when the lights came back on, a lawyer was dead.

SUSPECTS

OFFICER COPPER

She looks back on her days of being an RA. Not fondly, she just looks back. She's a lot happier now as a police officer, where she can both serve the cause of justice and commit crimes without being punished.

5'5" • RIGHT-HANDED • BLUE EYES • BLOND HAIR • ARIES

CAPTAIN SLATE

No longer just an astronomy teacher, now she's an astronaut, and she is about to be the first woman to travel to the dark side of the moon, although she doesn't like her copilot . . .

5'5" • LEFT-HANDED • BROWN EYES • BROWN HAIR • AQUARIUS

JUDGE PINE

Her experience being found guilty of murder in college has caused her to change her ways. As a judge, she's the one who gets to decide if someone is guilty or not!

5'6" • RIGHT-HANDED • BROWN EYES • BLACK HAIR • TAURUS

EX-CHANCELLOR OAK

Since he was expelled from his post as chancellor of Deduction College, he's found that people are taking his word a lot less seriously, and they're even doing wild things, like questioning him.

5'5" • LEFT-HANDED • GREEN EYES • GRAY HAIR • LIBRA

LOCATIONS

THE JURY DELIBERATION ROOM
INDOORS

Your best hope here is that one of the angry men is only angry for justice.

THE ACTUAL COURTROOM
INDOORS

This is maybe the best place to go if you want to see one person judge another.

THE JUDGE'S CHAMBERS
INDOORS

A nice desk, a good view out the window, and a closet filled with black robes.

THE PARKING LOT
OUTDOORS

More cop cars than Logico has seen since he got stuck behind that police parade.

WEAPONS

THE SCALES OF JUSTICE
HEAVY-WEIGHT • MADE OF METAL

Justice may be blind but it was because someone hit her with these scales.

A FLAG
LIGHT-WEIGHT • MADE OF POLYESTER

This wouldn't be the first time that someone was killed by/for a flag.

A GAVEL
MEDIUM-WEIGHT • MADE OF WOOD

Let's be frank: there's a reason they give the judge a big hammer. (Intimidation.)

A BAG OF CASH
HEAVY-WEIGHT • MADE OF CLOTH & PAPER

This is the kind of thing that you don't want to get caught with in court.

MOTIVES

 BECAUSE THEY KNEW THEY'D GET AWAY WITH IT

 AS A TRIAL RUN

TO PROVE THEIR AUTHORITY

 BECAUSE LOGIC DEMANDED IT

CLUES & EVIDENCE

- The person with a bag of cash would kill because they knew they'd get away with it.

- Officer Copper had not been in the parking lot.

- The person who wanted to prove their authority was in the judge's chambers.

- Whoever was in the jury deliberation room had a heavy-weight weapon.

- Ex-Chancellor Oak was seen waving a flag.

- The tallest suspect brought the scales of justice.

- The suspect who knew they would get away with it was found indoors.

- Whoever might kill as a trial run had brown hair.

STATEMENTS

(Remember: The murderer is lying. The others are telling the truth.)

Officer Copper: Mysteriously, Judge Pine did not bring a gavel.

Captain Slate: The person in the courtroom would not kill as a trial run.

Judge Pine: The scales of justice were not in the parking lot.

Ex-Chancellor Oak: Whoever had the flag would kill to prove their authority.

SUSPECTS   MOTIVES   LOCATIONS

WEAPONS

LOCATIONS

MOTIVES

WHO?

WHAT?

WHERE?

WHY?

49. AN OLD CRIME IN NEW AEGIS

Finally, Deductive Logico traveled to a city called New Aegis, where he felt a strong, unexplainable pull. Probably some kind of magnetic field, he reasoned. But when someone was murdered in seemingly impossible circumstances, he wondered if there was something more going on.

SUSPECTS

MAYOR HONEY

He managed to get himself elected mayor of this town. One of the things he learned from Deduction College was not to come up with elaborate schemes but just to promise people money.

6'0" • LEFT-HANDED • HAZEL EYES • BROWN HAIR • SCORPIO

CEO INDIGO

He is poking around this town and examining all the infrastructure. Nobody knows why, though.

5'11" • RIGHT-HANDED • GREEN EYES • BROWN HAIR • TAURUS

DR. SEASHELL, DDS

He has invented a mystic understanding of the universe, which he calls the Cosmiverse. He has also become a dentist.

5'7" • RIGHT-HANDED • GREEN EYES • GRAY HAIR • PISCES

SIR RULEAN

Okay, Logico is a little unsure if he believes the Official Knighting Documents that Rulean has in his possession. After all, they do seem a little like all the other qualifications he's claimed.

5'8" • RIGHT-HANDED • BLUE EYES • RED HAIR • LEO

LOCATIONS

THE TOWN SQUARE
OUTDOORS

A bustling town square filled with tourists, New Agers, UFO enthusiasts, and con artists.

THE SONIC OSCILLATOR
INDOORS

A giant dome out in the desert that purports to concentrate psychic energies but definitely concentrates money from rich people.

A UFO CRASH SITE
OUTDOORS

This just happened like a week ago and there is already an attempt to set up a tourist site around it. Logico thinks it was just a weather balloon.

A CRYSTAL SHOP
INDOORS

The best and most expensive place to buy crystals in the entire world.

WEAPONS

OUIJA BOARD
LIGHT-WEIGHT • MADE OF METAL

The most powerful magic artifact you can buy at a toy store.

A DECK OF MAROT CARDS
LIGHT-WEIGHT • MADE OF PAPER

You can use these murder-themed tarot cards to read your future.

AN IMPOSSIBLE TRIANGLE
LIGHT-WEIGHT • MADE OF OIL

There it was again. That impossible object. And yet, it was there. How?

A CRYSTAL BALL
HEAVY-WEIGHT • MADE OF CRYSTAL

If you look into it, it will tell you your future, so long as your future is a crystal ball.

MOTIVES

 TO STAY IN POWER

 TO SHOW OFF

TO PROVE THEIR
THEORY

TO PROTECT THEIR
SECRET PLANS

CLUES & EVIDENCE

- A fortune-telling card was found beside what is either a UFO or a weather balloon.

- Whoever was at a crystal shop was left-handed.

- The person who wanted to prove their theory was in the sonic oscillator.

- The second shortest suspect had never been in the town square.

- The suspect who wanted to stay in power was found indoors.

- A toy store receipt was seen indoors.

- Dr. Seashell, DDS, had a weapon that resembled the constellation made from these stars: W19 F7 P9 Q8 F4, J9 G3 F4 M8 E3, and L7 F1 E3 A4 P9. (See Exhibit E.)

STATEMENTS

(Remember: The murderer is lying. The others are telling the truth.)

Mayor Honey: The Ouija board was not in the sonic oscillator.

CEO Indigo: Dr. Seashell was not at a crystal shop.

Dr. Seashell, DDS: Whoever had the crystal ball wanted to show off.

Sir Rulean: CEO Indigo was in the town square.

SUSPECTS   MOTIVES   LOCATIONS

WEAPONS

LOCATIONS

MOTIVES

_____ **WHO?**

_____ **WHAT?**

_____ **WHERE?**

_____ **WHY?**

50. CONFRONTATION AT THE ALUMNI DINNER

Deductive Logico stormed into the alumni dinner, attended by the chancellor and the entire Council of Deans. He got everyone's attention by announcing that someone had been encouraging all the murders. They had manipulated everything, exactly according to plan.

SUSPECTS

INSPECTOR IRRATINO

The ringleader of the Intuitive Inquisition, expelled without a degree, but was he falsely accused? Or was he correctly accused?

6'2" • LEFT-HANDED • EMERALD-GREEN EYES • GREAT BROWN HAIR • AQUARIUS

CHANCELLOR TUSCANY

She is the best and most illustrious chancellor the school has ever had. Beloved by the students, loved by the faculty, and the focus of several magazine puff pieces, which have all praised her administration and the way she's turned the school around.

5'5" • LEFT-HANDED • GREEN EYES • GRAY HAIR • LIBRA

COACH RASPBERRY

Despite being a murderer, he has found a great career as a professional coach, although he's moved on to sports more popular than chessboxing. (Like pickleball!)

6'0" • LEFT-HANDED • BLUE EYES • BLOND HAIR • ARIES

DAME OBSIDIAN

Was inviting a pseudo confessed murderer to campus a good idea? Maybe not. Unless you're measuring it economically, because the bookstore sold a lot of copies.

5'4" • LEFT-HANDED • GREEN EYES • BLACK HAIR • LEO

LOCATIONS

OLD MAIN
INDOORS

Emphasis on the "old." This building is full of history and asbestos.

THE QUAD
OUTDOORS

They say it's designed to corral student rioters in the event of unrest.

THE ARBORETUM
OUTDOORS

This used to be the best place on campus to hang out. Now, honestly? It's the worst.

THE CHESSBOXING GYM
INDOORS

Just because this was at the center of a murderous scheme doesn't mean it can't be again.

HOW THEY MANUPULATED PEOPLE

WHAT HAPPENED AT DEDUC-TION COLLEGE: A YOUDUNIT
MEDIUM-WEIGHT • MADE OF PAPER

By calling this novel entirely fictional, she was able to make a fortune on slander.

A GARNET PIN
LIGHT-WEIGHT • MADE OF METAL & A GEMSTONE

Logico knows the secret behind these pins now, and he can tell garnets from rubies, too.

AN IVORY SCEPTER
HEAVY-WEIGHT • MADE OF IVORY

This plays an important part in the graduation ceremonies. It's worth its weight in ivory.

THE CHAMPIONSHIP TROPHY
HEAVY-WEIGHT • MADE OF METAL

This is the one they won twelve years ago. It's actually starting to rust now.

MOTIVES

 TO WIN, WIN, WIN

 TO DESTROY THE COLLEGE

FOR PUBLICITY

TO TAKE OVER THE SCHOOL

CLUES & EVIDENCE

- Logico was passed an anonymous tip that read: "IX XIV XIX XVI V III XX XV XVIII IX XVIII XVIII I XX IX XIV XV XXIII I XIX XIX V V XIV IX XIV XX VIII V XVII XXI I IV." (See Exhibit A.)

- The second tallest suspect was seen with the weapon made only of metal.

- The shortest suspect had a medium-weight weapon.

- The ivory scepter was found indoors.

- The person who wanted to take over the school was at Old Main.

- The person with a book wanted publicity.

- The suspect who wanted to win, win, win was in a building connected to the chancellor's mansion through the underground tunnels. (See Exhibit D.)

STATEMENTS

(Remember: The murderer is lying. The others are telling the truth.)

Inspector Irratino: Chancellor Tuscany always wanted to take over the school.

Chancellor Tuscany: The ivory scepter was at the chessboxing gym.

Coach Raspberry: Chancellor Tuscany was at Old Main.

Dame Obsidian: Coach Raspberry wanted to win, win, win.

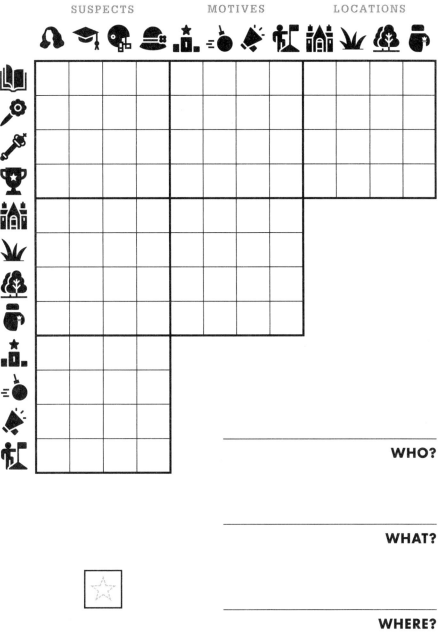

WHO?

WHAT?

WHERE?

WHY?

APPENDIX A

EXCERPTS FROM THE COURSE CATALOGUE OF DEDUCTION COLLEGE

FOUNDATIONS OF THE TRIVIUM

LOGIC 101. You start with what "is" means and you work your way all the way to "not."

RHETORIC 101. Starting with Aristotle and working our way to old French président Amaranth, you'll learn the basics of public speaking. The final assignment is to convince the professor to give you a good grade.

GRAMMAR 101. In this class, you will learn the skills you need to become extremely obnoxious.

TRIVIUM ELECTIVES

HOW TO WHIP PEOPLE UP (RHT 220). As a public speaker, few tasks are more important than whipping people up. Apathy is your greatest enemy, and this class will teach you how to slay your foe. Special significance is given to finding a common enemy. *Pre-req: RHT 101.*

CALMING DOWN MOBS (RHT 230). This is the only task more important than whipping people up, and to be honest, this is the one that's more likely to save your life. Anybody can whip people up, but getting an angry mob to step back and reconsider its actions . . . that's rhetoric! *Pre-req: PRC 101.*

COMMON MISTAKES AND HOW TO CORRECT THEM (GRM 210). Learn the most likely grammatical errors that your peers will make and how to correct them gently and pretentiously. *Pre-req: GRM 101, PRC 101.*

FOUNDATIONS OF THE QUADRIVIUM

GEOMETRY 201. You'll learn everything you've always wanted to know about triangles, and (to be honest) a whole bunch you never wanted to know. *Pre-req: LGC 101, RHT 121, GRM 131.*

ASTRONOMY 211. They're over your head, but it doesn't have to be over your head. The final class involves a field trip to a nearby hilltop to watch a meteor shower, which is a pretty iconic collegiate experience that you won't want to miss. *Pre-req: LGC 101, RHT 121, GRM 131.*

ARITHMETIC 221. It starts with one plus one but it gets a lot bigger than that. *Pre-req: 101, 121, 131.*

MUSIC 231. Learn the relationships between the notes, both their exact mathematical interrelationships, but also how they feel, groove-wise. *Pre-req: LGC 101, RHT 121, GRM 131.*

QUADRIVIUM ELECTIVES

A SURVEY OF CIRCLES (GMT 224). If it rolls, we'll talk about it. This covers all the basics of circles, from how to figure out how big they are, to how to figure out how round they are. A single percentage point of extra credit will be given to you for every digit of pi you can recite. *Pre-req: GMT 201.*

LINES AND YOU 202. A line is a series of points that stretches on into infinity. We won't be able to cover all of that in one semester, but we'll try. *Pre-req: GMT 201.*

THE LIFE AND SECRETS OF PYTHAGORAS (ARITH 223). Learn about the ancient Greek philosopher who worshipped numbers and refused to eat beans because he was afraid of being reincarnated as one. (Yes, Dame Obsidian did write a whodunit set in his school. No, we will not be reading it.) *Pre-req: ARTH 221.*

THE DRUMS: INSTRUMENT OR NOT? (MSC 255). We'll hear from both sides in this contentious discussion. On the one hand, they do make noise in a rhythmic way. On the other hand, no notes? Well, we'll have a lot of notes as we cover this. *Pre-req: MSC 231.*

A SURVEY OF CONSTELLATIONS (ASTRO 232). Have you ever looked up at the stars and thought, I wonder what that one is? Well, wonder no more, because by the time you've finished this class, you'll be able to identify all of them with ease. We'll start with the North Star and go from there. *Pre-req: ASTR 211.*

THE MUSIC OF CAMPUS (MSC 244). From the chirping of birds to the chattering of squirrels to the bell tower of Old Main, we'll study the tones, pitches, and rhythms of campus life. Experience reading sheet music is a must. *Pre-req: MSC 221.*

ADVANCED STAR POSITION CALCULATION (AST 401). In this class, you'll learn to calculate the precise positions of the stars in the sky. Then, we'll go out on a hill at the end of the semester and have a star-watching party, and we'll check to see how close everybody gets. Your final grade will be determined by how well you estimate your star's position and by the snacks you bring to the star-watching party. *Pre-req: ASTR 211, ARITH 221.*

PRACTICALIUM

CHESSBOXING BASICS (CHS 101). Frequently our most popular class, Chessboxing Basics teaches the foundations of our official school sport. Learn several defensive combinations and attacking strategies in both disciplines that underlie this sport. *Pre-Req LGC 101.*

MYSTERY WRITING (MYS 101). Visiting lecturer Dame Obsidian is teaching a small class on how to write a bestselling murder-mystery novel. Deduction College takes no responsibility for either the contents of this course or its health and safety features. *Pre-req: LGC 101.*

AN ARTICLE PUBLISHED BY DAME OBSIDIAN IN THE SCHOOL NEWSPAPER

I know that many of the students, faculty, and staff of Deduction College have expressed some concerns about my invitation to campus and being asked to lead a workshop. Doubtless, while some of those criticisms were valid, others were clearly motivated by bad faith, or, even worse, poor literacy. I am, as many people know, a writer of fiction, and all of my books are fictional, including *How I Murdered My Husband: An Idunit.*

Do I recognize that my lead detective, Lady Blackstone, bears a more than striking resemblance to myself, as she is an author whose husband goes missing under mysterious circumstances connected to a greenhouse in her backyard?

I do, of course, but I don't think those similarities are enough to make you think that I murdered my husband, buried his body in the backyard, and then built a greenhouse over it—that's ridiculous.

This confusion—between fact and fiction—is a hallmark of the age in which we find ourselves. An age in which readers cannot distinguish between the pages of a book and the world in which they live. No one should think that just because a novelist writes about a subject they therefore are living the lives of their characters, having the thoughts of their characters, committing the murders of their characters.

"Dame Obsidian is a murderer!" is what they say. I expect some of these people, were they alive when he was writing, would have read the first line of *Moby-Dick* and then wondered why the cover said that Herman Melville wrote the novel and not "Ishmael."

Luckily, Herman Melville would not have been in danger if someone mistook him for a fisherman; however, I cannot say the same.

Last night, someone threw a rock through the window of my on-campus cottage, clearly indicating that they did not find me welcome at this school.

Do not worry: I have no plans of going anywhere. Obsidian is hard to break.

I'll stay right here on campus and teach my class on mystery writing, and hope that, through my example, I can make a point to everyone. There is nothing that can stop you, so long as you believe in yourself.

And to the student who threw the rock through the window, I have one message. Great arm! A talent like that would perhaps be more beneficial on the chessboxing team. I think, if you'll read these words carefully, you'll understand that what I am saying to you is true: I am not a murderer; I have never murdered anyone; I will never murder anyone.

Now do you understand?

IRRATINO'S NOTE

Ξαπδ θνΩΥθδαδ,

σΔΥ πδα φαδαλσ θνβθταΞ τΔ ιΔθν τφα
θντΥθτθβα θνΩΥθεθτθΔν.

κα πδα π εαγδατ εΔΓθατσ τφπτ εααγε τφα
τδΥτφ τφδΔΥηφ πνσ μαπνε ναΓαεεπδσ.

κα λαψθαβα θν τφα ρψπεφ Δρ θνεθηφτ, τφα
μσετθΓ βθεθΔν, τφα θνΩΥθεθτθβα θντΥθτθΔν.

κα λαψθαβα σΔΥ Γπν λαψθαβα κφπταβαδ σΔΥ
κπντ τΔ λαψθαβα.

πνΞ τφπτ κφπταβαδ σΔΥ κπντ τΔ λαψθαβα θε
τδΥα λαΓπΥεα σΔΥ λαψθαβα θτ.

λαρΔδα κα Γπν ταψψ σΔΥ μΔδα, σΔΥ μΥετ
ιΔθν ΔΥδ δπνγε.

δατΥδν τφθε τΔ τφα ζαδεΔν κφΔ ηπβα θτ τΔ
σΔΥ, πψΔνη κθτφ σΔΥδ πνεκαδ.

μσεταδθΔΥεψσ σΔΥδε,
τφα ΓΥδδαντ ψαπΞαδ Δρ τφα θ.θ.

APPENDIX D
POP QUIZ

Can you answer the following questions about Deduction College? In order to graduate, students are asked to pass a series of increasingly difficult exams.

1. **Who was the founder of Deduction College?**
   a) Viscount Eminence
   b) Old Rosy Garnet
   c) Lord Graystone
   d) Lord Violet

2. **Who was the first student to attend the school?**
   a) Baron Maroon
   b) Chancellor Oak
   c) Viscount Eminence
   d) Secretary Celadon

3. **How many years before Logico graduated Deduction College did the school chessboxing team last win the chessboxing championship?**
   a) 2
   b) 5
   c) 10
   d) 11

4. **What is the real reason you aren't supposed to talk under the Silent Archway?**
   a) Sixty-four years of bad luck
   b) A nearby professor hates noise
   c) Echoes reverberate dangerously
   d) No real reason at all, just something people say

5. **What black-and-white animal is the mascot of Deduction College?**
   a) Zebra
   b) Penguin
   c) Siberian tiger
   d) Dalmatian

"SCORE: ___ / 5"

1. C
Lord Graystone founded Deduction College. (See Case 1: The Case of the Interrupted Tour.)

2. C
Viscount Eminence was the first student. (See Case 31: The Tragic Fate of Lord Graystone.)

3. D
The cheesboxing trophy was last won ten years before Logico's junior year, making it eleven years before his graduation year. (See Case 21: The Dead Can't Vote (Or Can They?).)

4. B
A nearby professor invented that legend because he hates noise. (See Case 16: The Stayover Slaying.)

5. B
The penguin is the official mascot of Deduction College: like logic, they're formal! (See Case 1: The Case of the Interrupted Tour.)

184

THE FINAL LETTER

You may find it easier to read this note in the mirror. This is intentional, because it illustrates the true nature of the school and helps to reveal my final lesson to you.

You have been taught that Lord Graystone founded the Deduction College, and that he cared only about logic. And you have been told that Old Rosy Garnet founded the Intuitive Inquisition, and that he cared only of his mystic dreams.

But Lord Graystone and Old Rosy Garnet both cared about logic and mysticism equally, because Lord Graystone and Old Rosy Garnet are, in fact, the same person: they are I.

When I founded the school, I saw that logic only worked when it was wholly unclouded by mysticism, and mysticism only worked when it was completely unfettered by reason. To mix the two is to court disaster, but to rely on only one is the height of foolishness.

Logic alone is rigid and dogmatic. Mysticism is too passionate and wild. They both must work together, controlling and harnessing each other. And so, I founded the Deduction College to search for truth in a rigorous way, and I founded the Intuitive Inquisition to question that truth.

To demonstrate this, I have left three pieces of proof, for seekers who wish to learn:

One is the engraving beneath the statue of me in the quad. You will see a message advocating logic. But look at the first letter of every sentence, and you will see a different message: REBEL. Read the lines from the bottom up, and you will see a different message entirely.

And examine the tunnels, built for the purpose of the Inquisition. If you view them from up north, with one eye closed, you shall see my signature written in their every curve: GRAYSTONE.

And finally, if you take the letters of my name, LORD GRAYSTONE, and rearrange them, then you will find they spell another name, as well: OLD ROSY GARNET.

And that is why it was said that Old Rosy Garnet killed Lord Graystone. As I grew older, I found the pleasures of logic more exhausting, and less rewarding, while the joys of the esoteric felt greater and more pressing. And so I simply killed off one of my two selves, and lived out the rest of my days as Old Rosy Garnet, a quiet kook, suspected of murder, but enjoying his retirement. And now, at the end of my days, I am writing you this letter, to be passed down through the ages.

Do not forsake logic, and do not dismiss the esoteric. Both have something to teach.

Please take this lesson to heart! It is the final one I will teach in my life, and the last one you will learn from Deduction College. Now, you may consider yourself a true graduate. Congratulations.

HINTS

1. Logico checked his pockets and found a note that read, "Welcome to Deduction College, Logico. We'll be watching you! (P.S. Chancellor Oak never leaves Old Main.)"

2. Logico found another unsigned note in his backpack: "You're a promising candidate, and Whiz-Kid Night was in the cafeteria."

3. Written on the white board on the door was a message: "Straight-A Crimson was in the extra space. We're watching!"

4. On one of the corkboards in the Old Main hallways was a message that read, "Logico—the bell tower is mentioned in the description of MSC 244 (The Music of Campus) in Appendix A. You have great potential!"

5. Logico found another note slipped into his pocket: "Sure, 1=I, 2=II. But have you considered that 1=A and 2=B, as well? Signed, the 2."

6. According to a letter inside a mysterious envelope marked with two eyes, Champion Gold was seen with boxing gloves.

7. The chancellor's phone rang, and when Logico answered it, a voice told him that they had seen Assistant Professor Tuscany standing outside on the balcony in the rain—then they hung up. Then they called back and said they were watching him.

8. When Logico finally got the napkin straightened out, it read "COF-FEE SHOP CHALK HAD A TEXTBOOK." And there were two eyes drawn below it.

9. Logico looked out the window and saw a message written in the arrangement of hundreds of small candles placed on the quad below: "Dean Celadon was at the table of deans." What kind of resources did these people have?

10. Logico had a dream the night before this case, and in the dream, he saw the person who was writing him these love notes. And it was exactly who he thought it was. (Also, the dream person told him that Chancellor Oak was at home in his mansion.)

11. Written on Logico's class application was a note in that unknown handwriting: "MFA Candidate Gainsboro was seen searching Dame Obsidian's bookshelves."

12. Written on a slip of paper, tucked into a pew, was the following message beside a drawing of two eyes: "Can you see the hymnal in the stained glass?"

13. Logico heard a voice whispering from the shadows: "Can you see the carnivorous plant in the windows of the church?" When he tried to chase after it, all he caught was the sight of a robe disappearing into the darkness.

14. According to an anonymous classified ad in the paper, the classic newspaper-wrapped crowbar was in the bullpen. That's a strange classified ad. How do you even answer it?

15. Logico overheard someone say that if you wanted to tell the seats apart, it might help to label them on the page.

16. "When someone eats quickly, they are scarfing!" said the note Logico received. And then, for some reason, they had written, "Aye, aye, captain!"

17. Someone slipped Logico a note that read, "Whiz-Kid Night was using a fountain pen to go over those numbers. Do not forget that we're watching you!"

18. Logico found a note scrawled in the margins of an incredibly expensive book: "Dame Obsidian was in the line for autographs, trying to pretend that she wasn't herself in order to escape."

19. Someone had already written a message in the margins of Dame Obsidian's novel: "Loved the scene with the red herring in the (un)stained glass window."

20. Unfortunately, for this one, nobody gave Logico a hint.

21. One registration card simply said, "Hello again, Prospective: Candidate Red was seen vandalizing the statue of Lord Graystone."

22. An opinion poll found—with a 3 percent percent margin of error—that a political sign was in the old dorms.

23. Logico found a note written in one of his own books: "Prospective, the previous letter code is simple: each letter is replaced by the one before it."

24. Nobody knows who started the rumor, but there was one going around that the old chessboxing trophy was in the weight room. And Logico saw two eye drawings drawn on everything.

25. A message was discovered written in small stones on the arboretum

floor: the person who was planning to frack (and/or mine crypto) was in the formerly mysterious building.

26. Logico had a dream that Candidate Honey was at the center podium. People wearing robes were standing all around him. It was freaky (but prophetic).

27. The heavy bag was found in the equipment closet, according to a message written in the steam on the mirror, next to (once again) two eyes.

28. Scrolling across a screen that displayed announcements was this one: "The suspect with the same height as Straight-A Crimson was seen hanging around in the president's office."

29. Everybody was chanting: "GO GO, CENTER LOGICO!!" (But who started the chant?)

30. Logico saw someone at the after party wearing a robe. When he approached them, the person said that whoever wanted to win an election was in the chessboxing gym.

31. A scrap of paper much newer than the rest said that Earl Grey was inspecting the cube under construction.

32. Logico noticed a brief note scrawled on the tunnel map. It said, "The astronomy building connects with the student union."

33. Logico thought he heard voices whispering in the abandoned building, saying that the second tallest suspect was in the creepy basement.

34. The Great Heir Irratino looked great standing beside a family portrait. Also somebody had slipped Logico some kind of secret note but he wasn't paying attention.

35. Scribblings on one of the pages confirmed that Sea Captain Salt had the ruby key.

Appendix C. Irratino's letter is another cryptogram. The first word is DEAR.

36. Johnny Bluesky had a moon rock, and he kept saying, "I am proud of moon landing because I am American." Like, he said it *a lot.*

37. A whisper from the woods told Logico that a motorized rake was by a newish gate.

38. In order to speak the secret language of High Latin, you simply add "us" after every consonant sound in the beginning or middle of a word, and at the end, you add "um." For example, "secret" would be "susecrusetum."

39. Logico couldn't look away from the impossible cube, or from the shortest suspect who was holding it.

40. Unfortunately, Logico didn't receive any hints here.

41. Logico didn't get a hint this time (obviously), but he had the strangest feeling that the shortest suspect had brought a booby-trapped fedora.

42. Still no hints, but Logico had a hunch that the person who wanted to create a pretext for going home was in the big tent.

43. Logico knew by the flights of the birds that Brother Brownstone was seen by the forbidden books.

44. Logico closed his eyes and pictured the first thing that came to mind: Bookie-Nominee Gainsboro in a spooky attic!

45. Logico could tell in his gut Mx. Tangerine was telling the truth. And Irratino could tell that he could tell. And Logico could tell that he could tell that he could tell. And so on.

46. Using his intuition, Logico could tell that Director Dusty wanted to get a great shot.

47. Logico had a great sense that Grandmaster Rose wanted to prove his own superiority.

48. Logico flipped a coin to learn that an imbalanced scale was in a robe-filled closet.

49. CEO Indigo had a crystal ball, which Logico learned by looking into a crystal ball.

50. Logico realized that it was true, Inspector Irratino did want to destroy the school. But why?

SOLUTIONS

1. "It was Partyboy Mango with the scarf in the quad!"

Chancellor Oak reviewed Logico's logic and said, "Boy, you show real promise." And for the first time in a long time, Logico felt like, for once, his talents were appreciated.

On the other hand, Partyboy Mango was expelled for murder.

> Chancellor Oak I the heavy tome I Old Main
> Rich Kid Champagne I a stuffed penguin I the combination coffee shop/bookstore
> **Partyboy Mango I a beautiful school scarf I the quad**

2. "It was Young Lady Violet with a logic textbook in the game room!"

The college typically had a very stern policy of expelling students who were guilty of murder, but in the face of Lady Violet's money, they were able to make an exception. (A stern exception.)

But that wasn't good enough for Lady Violet. "I still don't even like being *accused* of murder! Even if I did do it! Even if it was justified because they were making me wait!"

> **Young Lady Violet I a logic textbook I the game room**
> Shy Abalone I boxing gloves I the study room
> Whiz-Kid Night I a ruby pin I the cafeteria

3. "It was Cheater Rulean with a killer snake in the bedroom complex!"

"Oh, please, fine. I did it! But I had to do it. Because this is too small a bedroom complex for five people. For four people, it's at least habitable. That makes sense, right?"

Straight-A Crimson pointed out that now, only three people had to share it: Cheater Rulean was certainly going to be expelled.

> Straight-A Crimson | a poisoned textbook | the common area
> Rich Kid Champagne | an ice dagger | the bathroom
> **Cheater Rulean | a killer snake | the bedroom complex**

4. "It was Computer Nerd Indigo with an ivory scepter in the chancellor's office!"

Indigo was outraged. "Fine," replied Computer Nerd Indigo, "I'll go off and make millions, while the rest of you will be stuck here making cents." And, in fact, that's exactly what happened.

> **Computer Nerd Indigo | an ivory scepter | the chancellor's office**
> Chancellor Oak | the course catalogue | the grand steps
> Assistant Professor Tuscany | an old thesis | the bell tower

5. "It was Student President Pine with a hundred-dollar yo-yo by the statue of Lord Graystone!"

She tried to attack Logico for ruining her election campaign, but Logico was able to duck-and-weave his way out of it. He managed to attract the interest of the assistant chessboxing coach, but he lost the interest of the Mystery Boy, who seemed to disappear into the quad the moment the mystery had been solved.

> **Student President Pine | a hundred-dollar yo-yo | the statue of Lord Graystone**
> The Mystery Boy | a ruby pin | the big lawn
> Trailblazer Tangerine | a generic flying disc | the fountain

6. "It was Champion Gold with boxing gloves in the boxing ring!"
Champion Gold scoffed at the accusation. "That doesn't make sense. Why would I need to kill a chessboxing student? Particularly one on a scholarship? Because I was threatened by him? Because when I saw him box I thought he'd be bad at chess and when I saw him play chess I was devastated by the knowledge that my time as the champ was limited, that eventually, someone would come along and replace me, and that the only recourse I had against the otherwise irresistible force of time was to murder this up-and-comer before he had a chance to come up?"

"Okay, I didn't know the motive before," Logico said, "but that sounds like it, yeah."

> Prodigy Rose | a giant knight | the chess classroom
> Assistant Coach Raspberry | a calculator watch | the locker room
> **Champion Gold | boxing gloves | the boxing ring**

7. "It was Dean Celadon with a heavy coat in the dining hall!"
"This doesn't make any sense!" cried Dean Celadon. "If I can't be a dean anymore just because I murdered someone, then I'll have to go to a place where criminals are welcomed . . . Congress!"

"Congratulations, Logico!" Chancellor Oak declared. "You've kept our campus safe. For solving this murder, and many others, I'd like to grant you a Chancellor's Fellowship. From now on, you'll receive personal instruction from yours truly on the important issues facing deductive reasoning today. Plus, a hefty stipend."

Logico had been excited ever since he said "hefty stipend."

> Chancellor Oak | a priceless vase | the library
> Assistant Professor Tuscany | a silver silverware set | the balcony
> **Dean Celadon | a heavy coat | the dining hall**

8. "It was Cadet Coffee with a pot of boiling water by the outdoor display!"

"Okay, sure, I did it! But I was only following orders!"

"Nobody can give you orders to kill!" Logico said. "You're not even in the army yet, you're just in a university club."

"I was trying to prove I could only follow my orders! Doesn't that make sense?"

> Coffee Shop Chalk I a textbook on the trivium I the coffee bar
> **Cadet Coffee I a pot of boiling water I the outdoor display**
> The Mystery Boy I a gluten-free bagel I the textbook section

9. "It was Dean Celadon with a framed diploma at the table of deans!"

Dean Celadon replied, "Excuse me! Point of order! This conversation has not been added to the agenda, so it does not make sense to discuss it now. I refuse to skip ahead!"

Assistant Professor Tuscany turned to Logico and told him, "We need to go see the chancellor and tell him about this."

Freshman Logico replied, "You're right. But not for the reason you think."

> **Dean Celadon I a framed diploma I the table of deans**
> Assistant Professor Tuscany I a letter opener I the entrance
>   archway
> Dean Glaucous I a ruby pin I the giant window

10. "It was Chancellor Oak with the power of logic itself in the chancellor's mansion! And he did it to avoid admitting he was wrong!"

"Now, son," Chancellor Oak replied, "be careful with these sorts of wild accusations. They don't reflect well on your capacity for deductive reasoning. If you're going to jump to such an erroneous conclusion, how can we uphold you as a model student? How can we call you an Oak's Fellow?"

But Logico was not the type to leap to conclusions, and he laid out his reasoning in front of the Council of Deans:

"Chancellor Oak has mismanaged the finances of the school, which is why he was studying the accounting book (see Case 1: The Case of the Interrupted Tour). The new dorms obviously cost a fortune, way more than they could ever generate in meal plan money (see Case 2: The Dormitory of Death and Case 3: A Locked Dorm Mystery). And in his own mansion, several of the chancellor's books and silverware were missing, because he was selling them (see Case 7: The Chancellor's Classic Mansion Murder).

"Furthermore, the murder victims were expensive drains on the college's finances: for example, a chessboxer on an athletic scholarship (see Case 6: The Opening Position of the Body). He was cutting corners . . . literally!"

"Ridiculous!" Chancellor Oak exclaimed. "All these murders had their own perpetrators and their own reasoning. It just doesn't make sense!"

"Provided by you!" Logico exclaimed. "Each of the murderers justified their own crimes in their own words. However, I noticed that each of them, in their justification, used some variation of a particular turn of phrase: 'It just makes sense.' This turn of phrase, I'm sure everyone here realizes, is a particular one of Chancellor Oak's. And considering several of the murderers had recently spent time studying with you (see Case 4: Old Main, New Corpse), my accusation is that you used logic, rhetoric, and grammar to convince them all that they needed to kill, but without them realizing it was you who had convinced them. Those are my findings!"

"Bah!" Chancellor Oak exclaimed. "This is such a rudimentary exercise in rhetoric that I could point out twenty errors in your reasoning before lunch." He chuckled when he said this, as if he had just said something very amusing and definitive, and everybody else was silent.

Nobody believed that a freshman could outreason the chancellor.

But then a lone voice spoke up, "Then do it!"

"Do what?!" Oak huffed.

"Point out the errors in his reasoning. If you say he's wrong, then prove it."

"Well, it's simple . . ." Chancellor Oak replied. "You see . . . I mean . . . well, if you . . ." And finally, he slumped back in his chair and bowed his head and mumbled something.

"What was that?" Tuscany asked.

And he raised his voice this time and said, "He might be the reincarnation of the old crook Garnet, but he's right."

To that, there were gasps. The board was shocked. Not that Chancellor Oak had admitted to murder, but that he had finally admitted he was wrong.

"Come on, Logico," Associate Professor Tuscany said as she led him out of the chancellor's office. "I think the Council of Deans has a lot to discuss."

Did you figure out who was behind the murders? Give yourself an extra five stars if you did. Draw them around the one star, and you'll add them all up at the end.

> Assistant Coach Raspberry | the chessboxing gym | the old computer | to make the chessboxing team win again
> **Chancellor Oak | the chancellor's mansion | the power of logic itself | to avoid admitting he was wrong**
> Dean Glaucous | the arboretum | a framed diploma | to keep his job
> Assistant Professor Tuscany | Old Main | a heavy thesis | to take over the school

11. "It was MFA Candidate Gainsboro with *How I Murdered My Husband* by her bookshelves!"

"I was doing it for research," he cried. "How could I figure out who committed the impossible chapel murder without doing the appropriate research?"

Everyone agreed this was a worthwhile reason to commit murder, but they also agreed that they didn't want to have a murderer in class. So Gainsboro was kicked out, and he vowed revenge—in the form of a literary masterpiece they'd all be jealous of.

Meanwhile, Deductive Logico was admitted to Dame Obsidian's class. "You seem like you'd have a real knack for this: we're just going over a seemingly impossible murder that occurred on campus just last night."

Dame Obsidian | a can of gray paint | her balcony
Fan Ficcer Pearl | an old-timey typewriter | her writing desk
MFA Candidate Gainsboro | *How I Murdered My Husband* | **her bookshelves**

12. **"It was nobody with a bottle of oil on the nondenominational altar!"**

"How is that possible?" Dame Obsidian asked. And she assigned, as homework, for each of the students to come up with the best explanation for how it happened.

For extra credit this semester, see if you can solve it before Logico does!

Frat Bro Brownstone | a bottle of wine | the functional pews
Sorority Sister Lapis | a hymnal | the (un)stained glass window
Nobody | **a bottle of oil** | **the nondenominational altar**

13. **"It was Loner Snow with a flamethrower near the rusted gate!"**
"Argh! I've seen things in these woods. Things you wouldn't believe. Things I couldn't explain. People in dark robes chanting in unknown tongues. This place is too weird. I'm going to go live someplace normal, like the Madding Mountains of Drakonia."

Loner Snow | **a flamethrower** | **the rusted gate**
Whiz-Kid Night | a machete | a mysterious building
Botanist Onyx | a carnivorous plant | the hidden pond

14. "It was Photographer Dusty with the classic newspaper-wrapped crowbar in the bullpen!"

"Fine!" Photographer Dusty said. "I didn't need to go to college to be a photographer anyway. I'll drop out and pursue my art." Of course, he almost immediately found it impossible to pursue his art without also making money, so he packed up and moved to Hollywood.

> Junior Editor Ivory | a fake aspirational Bookie | the editor's office
> Foreign-Exchange Red | a sack full of metal letters | the storage room
> **Photographer Dusty | the classic newspaper-wrapped crowbar | the bullpen**

15. "It was Sorority Sister Lapis with a big foam finger in the in-between seats!"

"I can't believe y'all stopped the game for a little ol' murder in the stands! Some bloodsport! I should have done it during the chess portion. At least then people would've been distracted!"

> The Mystery Boy | a school pennant | the floor seats
> Astronomer Azure | an exploding hot dog | the cheap seats
> **Sorority Sister Lapis | a big foam finger | the in-between seats**

16. "It was Shy Abalone with an unopened present in the chessboxing gym!"

Shy Abalone admitted it. "Okay, fine! I did it! I killed them! And you want to know why? Because they got close to me. I'm not shy because I'm nervous around people, I'm shy because once I get to know someone, I hate them so much I have to murder them!"

Later, Logico opened the present, and inside, he found yet another ruby pin. Immediately, he raced over to the silent archway and confronted the Mystery Boy, who was easy to find because there was basically nobody on campus.

"What are these pins about?"

The Mystery Boy smiled at Logico and replied, "I'm afraid I couldn't say."

"Then at least tell me your name."

But the Mystery Boy just winked at him.

> Assistant Professor Tuscany | a beautiful scarf | the quad
> The Mystery Boy | another ruby pin | the silent archway
> **Shy Abalone | an unopened present | the chessboxing gym**

17. "It was the Incredibly Talented Blackstone with a modern typewriter on the stage!"

"Oh, so you're going to kick me out of Deduction College? That's no problem. I'll go write the Great Original Novel: the GON!" He continued screaming about the GON as he was being thrown out, and then Dame Obsidian went ahead with her announcement.

However, instead of revealing to everyone the identity of the vicious mastermind who was stalking their campus, she instead announced that it would be revealed in her upcoming book, which she had just written about her time on campus, entitled *What Happened at Deduction College: A Youdunit.*

> **The Incredibly Talented Blackstone | a modern typewriter | the stage**
> Whiz-Kid Night | a fountain pen | the seats
> Dame Obsidian | a piece of paper | the entrance

18. "It was Coffee Shop Chalk with a bundle of pencils at the checkout!"

"Fine! I did it! I killed them! But you know why?! Because they were trying to leave without paying. Can you imagine?!" The Council of Deans immediately terminated his contract, but Chalk didn't care. He knew what he was going to do. He was going to start the biggest chain of bookstores the world had ever seen. And just wait, you'll see what he does with it!

> **Coffee Shop Chalk** | **a bundle of pencils** | **the checkout**
> The Mystery Boy | Dame Obsidian's latest masterpiece | the sign out front
> Dame Obsidian | a big, giant sword | the line for autographs

19. "It was the Super Spooky Secretino with a ticking clock in the nondenominational church!"

This was absolutely ridiculous, Logico thought. Sure, the plotting was compelling and the mystery was wondrously macabre, and it ended up an amazing (and unbelievable) climax in a series of tunnels beneath campus, but the entire story was basically a frame-up of the Mystery Boy! And while he was mysterious, and he was obviously up to something, he didn't seem guilty of murder, at least not how Dame Obsidian described it.

This was absolutely ridiculous! It was one thing when she was claiming that she was a murderer in her books. It was another to claim it was someone else—especially when it wasn't! But fortunately for the Mystery Boy, Logico had solved the impossible chapel murder. Have you?

Logico slammed the book shut. He had suddenly realized two things: he knew why Dame Obsidian had accused the Mystery Boy, and he knew what to do about it.

> Boy Detective Blakenwitte | a red herring | Dame Obsidian's cottage
> **Super Spooky Secretino** | **a ticking clock** | **the nondenominational church**
> The Annoying Cinereous | stakes | the arboretum

20. "It was Dame Obsidian with the sword on the nondenominational altar. How? By painting herself like a statue!"

"Outrageous!" Dame Obsidian cried. "There's no proof!"

"And that's why you tried to frame that student for the crime! Because you saw him outside the church, through the (un)stained glass window, and you were afraid that he was the only witness to the crime. You had to tarnish his name—whatever it is—in order to guarantee that if he accused you, nobody would believe him."

"Oh, that's so ridiculous. You're another one of those who believes that I'm a murderer just because I write about murder."

"Well, yes, in part," Logico replied, "I just re-read the article that you published in the school newspaper, and if you read the first letter of the first word of every sentence, I notice there's quite a different message!" (See Appendix B.)

Did you figure out it was Dame Obsidian? If you did, give yourself one gold star. That's not a lot, but she was very, very suspicious.

Of course, after her crimes had been exposed, Dame Obsidian had to get out of town. Not because people didn't want her, but because so many people were eager to interview her about her cleverness that she was absolutely hounded by fans.

Her sales went through the roof. Both *What Happened at Deduction College: A Youdunit* and its sequel (*More of What Happened at Deduction College: A 2Dunit*) sold enormously well, and they proved that she could write about more than just murdering her husband. With that money, she was able to hire a crack team of lawyers that defended her against Logico's "spurious allegations."

But none of that had happened yet. At that moment, Logico was sitting on the steps of the Church of Reason, realizing he was unlikely to get a recommendation letter from Dame Obsidian. Mystery solving had its costs, he was thinking, when the Mystery Boy walked up to the bottom of the steps and called up to him.

"Hey."

"What do you want?" Logico said.

"Thanks for clearing my name," the Mystery Boy said.

"Why didn't you tell me you saw her do it?"

"I didn't. I saw a blur."

"Still. You should have said something."

"There are certain things I can't reveal about myself."

"Are there any things you can reveal?"

"Irratino," the Mystery Boy answered.

"What?" Logico replied.

"My name is Irratino."

Despite himself, Logico smiled.

"Nice to meet you, Irratino."

Frat Bro Brownstone | a bottle of wine | the functional pews | bro science

Sorority Sister Lapis | a hymnal | the (un)stained glass window | with smoke and mirrors

The Mystery Boy | a bottle of oil | the front steps | through a secret passage

Dame Obsidian | a giant sword | the nondenominational altar | painting themselves like a statue

21. **"It was Candidate Rulean with too big a bite at a nice spot in the grass. And his platform was more leniency for murderers!"**

"Look, we all know that if she was running, she'd beat us all! So I did what I had to do! Can you blame me?!"

Candidate Honey was outraged. "This is no way to win an election. It should go to the best person for the job!" The student voters applauded his anti-murder stance.

Rebel Umber | a ruby pin | a voter registration table | keeping things comfortably as they are

Candidate Red | the championship trophy | the statue of Lord Graystone | overturning the administration

Candidate Rulean | too big a bite | a nice spot in the grass | more leniency for murderers

> Candidate Honey | a coffee thermos | the sidewalk | fewer required courses

22. "It was Townie Taupe with a harpsichord in the new dorms. And he was wearing big, giant boots!"

"Fine!" shouted Townie Taupe. "I was sick of being asked who I was going to vote for, so I did something about it! If people know that I'm killing people, they probably won't try to poll me then, will they?"

Candidate Honey just shook his head. "This kind of thing is why I'm running for office."

> **Townie Taupe | a harpsichord | the new dorms | big, giant boots**
> Foreign-Exchange Red | a political sign | the old dorms | comfortable sneakers
> Candidate Honey | a political flyer | the sidewalk between them | fancy-pants loafers
> Trailblazer Tangerine | a beautiful textured jacket | the rooftop overlook | some sweet sandals

23. "It was Trailblazer Tangerine with the dictionary by the statue of Graystone. And they were ready to ****ing roll!"

Tangerine was clearly not sorry. "People are going to say I'm irrational! But when we look back on this, we'll understand it for what it was! Me being a trailblazer! One day, everyone will agree with me!"

Logico doubted that this was true. But he decided to remember it, just in case. Meanwhile, Candidate Honey made up a new speech on the spot, denouncing political violence and lauding Logico for all that he had done.

> **Trailblazer Tangerine | a dictionary | the statue of Graystone | ready to ****ing roll**

> Candidate Honey | the speech itself | the crowd below | bored
> out of their minds
> Straight-A Crimson | a letter opener | the fountain | Angry! Fu-
> rious! Inconsolable!
> The Mysterious Irratino | a megaphone | the big stage | open-
> minded as to what will be said

**24. "It was Hot Shot Maroon with a penknife in the chess library. And
he had solid, dependable positional play!"**

"Fine! I killed him! I wanted to be on the team so bad! I would have done
anything. I would have killed ten people."

"Ironically," Assistant Coach Raspberry said, "you would have made
the team if you hadn't committed murder, but now you're out. Logico,
step up. You're on the team."

Logico acted as nonchalant as he could until he was safely out of
sight. Then, he leapt up in the air and shouted, "Woo-hoo!" When he
landed, he saw that Irratino was watching him, so he tried to act cool
again. Mercifully, Irratino acted like he hadn't seen it.

> Assistant Coach Raspberry | an actual horse | the obstacle
> course | willing to risk it all every time
> Prodigy Rose | the ropes | the big loop | reeeally booked up on
> the openings
> Chessboxer Blaze | the old chessboxing trophy | the weight
> room | incredibly fast and fancy footwork
> **Hot Shot Maroon | a penknife | the chess library | solid, de-
> pendable positional play**

**25. "It was Ambitious Mauve with a regular ol' saw in the (for-
merly) mysterious building. And she wanted to frack and/or
mine crypto!"**

"Okay, fine! I did it! I killed them. But they were trying to unionize the volunteers. Then we never would have completed this project in time, and I wouldn't have been able to frack and/or mine crypto!"

Logico pointed out that now, she'd be expelled, and all her ambitions would go to waste.

"Well," she replied, "this is just the kick in the pants I need to get out of here and go fulfill my destiny in Silicon Valley! Do you know any computer nerds that are hiring?"

Ambitious Mauve | a regular ol' saw | the (formerly) mysterious building | fracking and/or crypto-mining
Rich Kid Champagne | some cool rocks | the no-longer-hidden pond | Theater. Immersive theater.
Botanist Onyx | a lawnmower | the beautiful gate | an animal rescue & coffee shop
Candidate Honey | a chainsaw | the cobblestone path | whatever people want to do

26. **"It was Moderator Grayscale with a microphone at the moderator table. And he said, 'Everybody, stop throwing things at each other!'"**

"Yes, I did it! I couldn't stand them all arguing! So I had to do something! And ultimately, what I had to do was kill somebody. Then, they knew I was serious, and we were able to get down to business."

Of course, nobody wanted to be moderated by a murderer! So the debate was called a tie. In a way, that's the goal of all moderators. So for him, it was a success.

Candidate Red | a dictionary | the left podium | "If we don't win with votes, we'll win through other means."
Candidate Honey | a fancy wristwatch | the center podium | "I'll promise you anything you want, and I'll try to deliver."

> Candidate Rulean | a giant pile of notecards | the right podium |
>   "My name is Candidate Honey, and I want to be your president."
> **Moderator Grayscale | a microphone | the moderator table |**
>   **"Everybody, stop throwing things at each other!"**

27. **"It was Assistant Coach Raspberry with the heavy bag in the equipment closet. And he loved *By Rook or Left Hook: How to Win at Chessboxing*!"**

"The book says that the winner is the person who is willing to do whatever it takes. And so I did! Logico, you'll thank me when you win the national championship."

And so, Assistant Coach Raspberry was kicked out of college coaching. However, his violent criminal past did not deter him from pursuing a career in the pros, which was very successful, albeit occasionally marred by the (credible) accusation that he would do anything to win.

> **Assistant Coach Raspberry | the heavy bag | the equipment**
>   **closet | *By Rook or Left Hook: How to Win at Chessboxing***
> Candidate Honey | a giant sword | the ducts | *The Bishop's in a*
>   *Box: A Dame Obsidian Mystery*
> The Mysterious Irratino | a framed photograph | the washrooms
> | *White and Black and Blue: A History of Chessboxing*
> Chessboxer Blaze | a chess clock | the lockers | *King of the*
>   *Ring: The Biography of a Champion*

28. **"It was Straight-A Crimson with an ivory scepter on the high balcony. And she thought Champion Gold would win!"**

"By Garnet's Curse, it was the right thing to do," she said. "I won't disclose my reasons. But I stand by my actions. If I'm kicked out of school, then so be it." So Straight-A Crimson kicked off her heels and moved to Drakonia to join the radicals fighting against the tsar.

Logico, meanwhile, got on the bus to the national chessboxing championship, and Irratino approached him.

"I know you'll sacrifice a queen to win. But will you sacrifice your values, too?"

"What are you talking about?" Logico asked.

"Oh," Irratino said, "you really don't know, do you?"

"What?" Logico replied. He really didn't.

But Irratino wouldn't tell him. Instead, he just said, "Good luck, Logico," and left it at that.

> Whiz-Kid Night | a ruby pin | the president's office | Prodigy Rose
> **Straight-A Crimson | an ivory scepter | the high balcony | Champion Gold**
> Candidate Honey | a trumpet | the courtyard | Logico, of course
> The Mystery Boy | a poisoned apple | the food court | Chessboxer Blaze

29. **"It was Junior Logico with a wild haymaker in the dead center. And he planned to dedicate his victory to the many murder victims."**

Logico knocked Champion Gold to the mat, and the ref counted him out. Logico won the national chessboxing championship, bringing home the trophy to Deduction College for the first time in a decade.

The crowd went wild. They were going mad. And there, at the front, was Candidate Honey, wearing a tuxedo, applauding and cheering as loudly as everyone else, as if it had been him who won, as well. But there, at the back of the arena, Logico saw Irratino, watching him.

And Logico knew what he needed to do.

> **Junior Logico | a wild haymaker | the dead center | to the many murder victims**

> Chessboxer Blaze | a solid right hook | out of the ring | to Deduction College
>
> Champion Gold | an inescapable checkmate | the corner | to themselves and their own glory
>
> Prodigy Rose | the ol' one-two | on the ropes | to everyone who ever doubted them

30. "It was Candidate Honey with the old chessboxing trophy in the chessboxing gym. Why? To win an election!"

"My chessboxing career simply went too easily to believe! First, why would Hot Shot Maroon need to kill someone to get on the team? (See Case 24: I Hope You Don't Get Cut.) As it was pointed out, he would have made the team without committing murder. And then, my former coach murdered my opponent right before I would have been eliminated (see Case 27: Before the Match, After the Murder).

"When Candidate Honey participated in the debates, he had fed the answers to Candidate Rulean, but their notecards got mixed up: that's why Rulean accidentally said that he was Candidate Honey! And we all just thought he was unintelligent. (See Case 26: The Debate of Death.)

"Candidate Honey had whipped up a fervor of school spirit in his speeches, and while he claimed to be a man of the people, he actually wore fancy watches no regular student could afford (see Case 23: Speaker for the Dead). And it turns out Trailblazer Tangerine was right! They knew what we didn't!

"Finally, when I won the national chessboxing championship with a wild haymaker, I knew that something was wrong. Champion Gold had specifically taught us how to avoid being hit by wild haymakers (see Case 6: The Opening Position of the Body), and yet I—a student who had barely made the team—was able to knock him out. It was too easy. That's when I knew.

"His goal was to identify himself with the school and the school's chessboxing team, particularly me. And then, if I won, he would ride that popularity to a new election. But I didn't win the boxing match fairly, so I must decline the championship, and withdraw my endorsement of Candidate Honey."

And so, Junior Logico's chessboxing career was over before it even began, and Candidate Honey's political career suffered a major setback. And though Logico knew he had done the right thing, he couldn't help feeling ashamed, or perhaps nostalgic, for a future that would never be.

But then, he saw—in the back corner of the arena—the Mysterious Irratino. And the Mysterious Irratino smiled at Logico and nodded at him, and the shame left Logico's heart. And it doesn't take a detective to understand why.

(Did you know it was Candidate Honey? If so, give yourself three extra stars.) And were you able to decode the message on the statue of Lord Graystone? Turn this book upside down to read it, and give yourself three stars if you decoded it correctly:

REMEMBER THESE WORDS
EVERYTHING MAY BE GRASPED WITH LOGIC
BANISH THE DELUSION THAT
ESOTERICISM HAS ITS PLACE
LET YOURSELF BE NOT DECEIVED

The Mysterious Irratino | a school pennant | the garden park | to get sweet, sweet revenge
Chessboxer Blaze | a beautiful scarf | the student union | as an accident during a match
Candidate Honey | the old chessboxing trophy | the chessboxing gym | to win an election
Candidate Red | the speech itself | the Greek Theatre | for bloody revolution

31. "It was Old Rosy Garnet with a bejeweled dagger in New Main!"
Yes, that's right: Lord Graystone was stabbed in the back by a bejeweled

dagger, and the authorities never caught his perpetrator. But it was clear that Old Rosy Garnet was responsible.

Ever since then, Old Rosy Garnet has been a sort of devil for the school, a mischievous force invoked when things don't go your way. It's not uncommon to hear a student exclaim "Curse Old Garnet!" when they fail an exam.

But all of this is not the entire story, not by a long shot.

> Earl Grey | a school charter | a cube under construction
> First Student Eminence | a tablet | a big ol' field
> **Old Rosy Garnet | a bejeweled dagger | New Main**

32. "It was Botanist Onyx with a commemorative pen in the abandoned building!"

"Okay! You can prove I was lying, but I wasn't lying because I'm a murderer. I was lying because I thought if I told you what I saw, you wouldn't believe me!"

"What did you see?" Logico asked.

"There were people in robes and masks," she said, "and they were sneaking around the abandoned building. And I saw the missing alumnus! Look! I made a sketch of it with this pen!"

She showed Logico the sketch she had made. Like her drawings of plants, it was mesmerizingly good. But it didn't prove anything. Logico turned to the Mysterious Irratino and said, "Stay right here. I'm going to go into that abandoned building to investigate."

> Full Dean Tuscany | a bottle of a prohibited beverage | the astronomy building
> **Botanist Onyx | a commemorative pen | the abandoned building**
> The Mysterious Irratino | a leather-bound dissertation | Rhetoric Hall

33. "It was RA Copper with a wooden baton in the creepy basement!"

"Fine! I killed them! But they were breaking the rules! They were down in here, wearing robes and ignoring the orders of an RA. So, I hit them with this wooden baton. And then, when they continued to resist, I hit them a bunch more. Finally, they stopped resisting."

RA Copper gestured over to where the robed body had been, but it was gone. RA Copper was glad she wasn't in trouble for murder, but she was upset that a rule-breaker had gotten away.

Only one clue remained: a piece of paper with a map, seemingly of tunnels that existed beneath Deduction College. (See Exhibit D.) What was this?

Logico knew the one person he needed to talk to about this. He stormed back outside the abandoned building and right up to the Mysterious Irratino, who was still waiting where Logico had left him. "What's going on?" he demanded, waving the map. "What do you know?"

"Fine," Irratino said, "I'll tell you what I can."

Johnny Bluesky | a tiny bean-stuffed animal | the cobwebbed
classroom
Foodie Aubergine | a heavy black robe | the rickety rooftop
RA Copper | a wooden baton | the creepy basement

34. "It was Skeptic Seashell with a velvet-upholstered chair in the grand bedroom!"

"Yes," said Seashell, "I wanted to test Irratino's so-called psychic in-tuition. But the fact that you caught me proves everything I believed is wrong. I must go and think on this and determine a new model of the cosmos."

Irratino said that, on account of his butler being dead, he would go himself to make tea. While he waited, Logico had a look around. First, he stared at the painting of Irratino and his two moms. Then, he rifled through the papers on the table.

> Skeptic Seashell | a velvet-upholstered chair | the grand bedroom
> Whiz-Kid Night | a ship in a bottle | the grand fireplace
> The Great Heir Irratino | a family portrait | the grand deck

35. "It was Sea Captain Salt with the ruby key on a ship at sea!"

And that's the story of how he became the Great Heir Irratino. For Irratino's two mothers were lost at sea, and the sea captain returned with a story of a shipwreck and the claim that the ruby key had been left on the island. But when the ruby key was discovered in the sea captain's safe, it was clear that he had lied, and that surely, he had been responsible for the deaths of Irratino's mothers.

Irratino entered with the tea, and Logico pretended not to be studying these private papers, but he could not hide how he felt, and he told Irratino, "I'm sorry."

"I appreciate it, Logico," Irratino said, and he handed him a cup of tea and a note, written in a secret code. "But if you're so interested in solving a mystery, then I have another one for you."

With that, he handed Logico a letter. Try to decode it in Appendix C. See the Hints if you're stuck.

> Sea Captain Salt | the ruby key | a ship at sea
> Irratino's Mother | a signet ring | the open ocean
> Irratino's Other Mother | a silver locket | Amaranth Island

36. "It was Astronomer Slate with a book of star names under the shady tree!"

"We got into an argument about the stars! He was telling me some kind of nonsense about the placement of the stars in the sky, that they were moving around in strange, impossible ways, and well, one thing led to another, and yeah, I did it. Fine! I resign as a teacher!"

Logico couldn't wait for this murderer to finish her customary monologue, because he wanted to tell Irratino his response to the letter: "I'm not joining. Yet. But I want to hear more."

"Of course you do, Logico."

Irratino took Logico away from the other students, and they wandered beneath the stars while they talked.

"Logico, you need to see to believe. But to truly see, you must first believe."

"You can believe whatever you want today and whatever you want tomorrow. But when I know something to be true, with reason, it will still be true in a thousand years."

"Are you sure about that, Logico? Come with me."

Johnny Bluesky | a moon rock | a parked car
Astronomer Slate | a book of star names | the shady tree
The Great Heir Irratino | a telescope | the grassy knoll

37. "It was Pet Person Cloud with a killer snake by the great stone cube!"

Pet Person Cloud agreed to turn himself in, and Logico and Irratino said they'd make sure he did it. Irratino rushed him away, and then ran his hands along the giant stone cube.

"Wait a second," Logico said, "do you know the secret of this cube?"

Irratino smiled. He reached into his jacket and pulled out a ruby key. "I do." He turned and ran it along the side of the cube, and when he had found a particular spot on the smooth stone, he inserted the key, and it clicked into an imperceptible mechanism. Irratino turned it, and it clicked again.

The stone cube began to open up. A door unfolded from the side of it like an origami flower. It seemed like magick, but Logico knew it must have been some sort of mechanism. Inside was a set of stairs, leading down into endless darkness.

"Come with me," Irratino said, "to explore the unknown."

Whiz-Kid Night | a pop quiz | the weedy path
Townie Taupe | a motorized rake | the newish gate
Pet Person Cloud | a killer snake | the great stone cube

38. "It was 'Philosopher' Bone with a pouch of magick powders by the giant portrait!"

"You're kicked out of the club!" Irratino exclaimed to "Philosopher" Bone. "Logico, I hope you won't think less of us because of this."

"Well, ignoring the murder, why are we passing through a creepy shrine to the mysterious founder?" Logico said.

"It makes an odd first impression, doesn't it." Irratino shook his head. "We were all weirded out by it at first. But when you understand, you'll understand. We all once didn't, and now we all do. Come. Follow me. And welcome to the inner chamber of the tomb!"

Logico really didn't like the sound of that.

Botanist Onyx | a secret handshake | the stone bust
"Philosopher" Bone | a pouch of magick powders | the giant portrait
The Great Heir Irratino | the ruby key | the sarcophagus

39. "It was Whiz-Kid Night with an impossible triangle in an enormous library!"

"I had to do it, Irratino! There's something happening down here! Realities are shifting! One thing is true one moment, and another at another moment!"

But Logico wasn't listening to them; instead, he was staring at the triangle. His brain could not comprehend it. It seemed wrong, somehow. But worse, it seemed like it wasn't the triangle that was wrong, but the rest of the world. This thing couldn't exist in a rational world. It was impossible, and yet it existed, so it must have been the world that was impossible—

And suddenly, he was standing in a void, looking across at the Mysterious Irratino.

"Where are we?" Logico asked. "What is this place?"

"We're not actually here," Irratino said. "We never were."

"What do you mean?"

"This is a memory, Logico. And you're remembering everything wrong. The more you think about these moments, the more different they are. You've thought about this time so many times, you've gotten the details wrong. We never spoke at Deduction College, did we?"

Logico thought, and his memories seemed like a kaleidoscope. One image overlapping the other, one story overlapping the next. But one stronger, more vivid than the others. Was it the truth?

"No," Logico said, "we never met. I was too shy. I saw you from across the quad, but I never said anything. I never even got your name. I should have asked your name."

"But we met later," Irratino said. "You still met me eventually."

"Not soon enough," Logico replied, and then—

Suddenly, he woke up in his dorm room. It was morning, and he would have thought the entire thing was a dream, except . . . there on his nightstand was a ruby pin. But he picked it up, and he realized, suddenly, and with great clarity, that it wasn't a ruby at all: it was a garnet.

He spent the first hour of his morning trying to decide what to do. And the second hour of his morning realizing he was late to graduation.

> **Whiz-Kid Night | an impossible triangle | the paradoxical library**
> The Great Heir Irratino | a strange fork | the ritual room
> Sociologist Umber | a bizarre cube | the collection of mystery

40. **"It was the Great Heir Irratino with the bejeweled dagger that proves he is the leader of the Intuitive Inquisition, which was founded by Old Rosy Garnet!"**

After the ceremony, Logico raced to Irratino and demanded, "How could you be the leader of a group founded by the murderer of the founder? You've been wearing garnets all around campus! It's horrific! And what's more, you lied to me about it!"

"I . . ." Irratino seemed to stammer. Finally he said, "You're right, I did."

Full Dean Tuscany stepped between the two of them before they came to blows. "It's okay, Logico. He lied to all of us. But we have to do the right thing. The *logical* thing."

And so the Great Heir Irratino was expelled just as he was set to graduate, and Logico, who did graduate, chose not to display his diploma. He put it in a folder and hid it, because although he appreciated knowing how to reason, he had lost so much.

He had lost the mentorship of Chancellor Oak. He'd lost a great teacher with Dame Obsidian. He'd lost the chessboxing championship, and his good friend Candidate Honey. And now, worst of all, he had lost Irratino.

Logico wondered if going to Deduction College was worth it in the end.

Was logic worth losing it all?

Before you solved this puzzle, did you figure out that Old Rosy Garnet founded the secret society? Or that the Great Heir Irratino was running it now? If so, give yourself three extra stars each.

Whiz-Kid Night | the Counting Club | a compass | First Student
   Eminence
Full Dean Tuscany | the Council of Deans | the ivory scepter |
   Lord Graystone
**The Great Heir Irratino | the Intuitive Inquisition | the ruby
   dagger | Old Rosy Garnet**
Tiny Taupe | the Tea Society | a commemorative mug | Earl Grey

**41. "It was Vice President Mauve with a red herring in New Aegis.
Why? To help with her career!"**

"Oh, but you think I was wrong to do it? My career is the most important thing to me! And if I have to sacrifice anything—including my reputation as a non-murderer—then I'm willing to do it, because you have to be willing to stand up for what you believe."

Logico agreed with the sentiment, but not with her conclusions. Hmm . . . was he being illogical?

> Viscount Eminence | a booby-trapped fedora | The Republic of Drakonia | to stop a revolution
>
> **Vice President Mauve | a red herring | New Aegis | to help with their career**
>
> Cosmonaut Bluski | a heavy codebook | Deduction College | to protect their secret identity
>
> Chancellor Tuscany | a golden bird | Hollywood | to maintain their power

42. **"It was Major Red with the Tiny Red Booklet near a twisted and mangled tree. Why? To instill fear in his troops!"**

"The logic of the situation demanded it. My troops were losing faith in me, and well, there're two ways to restore faith in an army's success. Write this down in the Tiny Red Booklet: The first is to have a great victory on the battlefield. We can't do that with a demoralized army, so I had to resort to the other method: fear. So, did you hear that everybody?! I killed him!"

Logico decided not to ask again about a donation.

> Radical Crimson | a silver bullet | the booby trap | to push the army leftward
>
> **Major Red | the Tiny Red Booklet | a twisted and mangled tree | to instill fear in his troops**
>
> Comrade Champagne | a stick of cheap dynamite | the big tent | to create a pretext for going home

> Militant Lead | a garland of garlic | a weird-looking rock |
> because he was following orders

43. "It was Sister Lapis with sacramental wine in the courtyard. Why? Because a voice told her to!"

"I did it because God willed it! I heard a voice, and the voice was the voice of God, and it told me to kill, and so I did! Doing anything else would betray my beliefs and my sense of good and evil, and I am a good person, so I didn't want to do that."

But then Bishop Azure pointed out to Sister Lapis that what she had actually heard was the TV, playing an old Midnight Mystery movie.

"Oh," she said, "well, in that case . . . oops?"

> **Sister Lapis | sacramental wine | the courtyard | because a
> voice told them to**
>
> Bishop Azure | a holy relic | the cliffs | to maintain their leadership role
>
> Father Mango | a poisoned goblet | the chapel | as part of a party gone bad
>
> Brother Brownstone | a heavy candle | the forbidden library | in order to leave the monastery

44. "It was Dame Obsidian with an axe in the great hall. Why? To write a bestseller!"

Dame Obsidian didn't seem surprised to be accused. She had asked Logico to solve the case, after all. "He was a horrible writer's assistant, and I knew my next book would be a flop unless I got a new one. But Logico, you've still got it! I'm impressed. As sharp now as you were in Deduction College. You know, you really were my favorite student. Would you be interested in being my new writing assistant?"

Logico politely excused himself and stepped outside before he was murdered, too. There, in the darkness, he looked up at the stars, and he hoped Irratino was looking at them, too.

> **Dame Obsidian | an axe | the great hall | to write a bestseller**
> Bookie-Nominee Gainsboro | a vial of poison | the spooky attic | to create art (lol, jk—for revenge)
> Editor Ivory | a booby-trapped fedora | the master bedroom | to make a million dollars
> Chairman Chalk | a fork | the grounds | to conquer publishing forever

45. "It was Officer Copper with a hypnotic pocket watch under the big gate. Why? Because she was getting bored!"

"Well, can you blame me?! All they do here is talk about the ineffable! It's intrinsically infuriating!" She stormed away, partially because of how mad she was, and partially to . . . you know, get away.

When she was gone, Irratino turned to Logico and began to say something, but Logico interrupted: "Are you mad at me?"

"For catching me in a lie? And getting me expelled from school just as I was about to graduate?" He paused. "I'm not mad," Irratino said. "Just disappointed."

"In what?"

"I would tell you, Logico. But I know you don't believe anything you don't see yourself."

"Are you saying the Intuitive Inquisition wasn't behind the murder of Lord Graystone?"

Irratino chuckled. "You'll figure it out without my help."

"But you've given me so much help in the past," Logico said. "All those hints . . ."

"What are you talking about?" Irratino said. "I haven't sent you any hints . . ."

Then who was doing it?

Mx. Tangerine | a selenite wand | the grand chateau | to steal
a really expensive artifact
Inspector Irratino | a poisoned candle | an impossible hedge
maze | to understand the cosmos
**Officer Copper | a hypnotic pocket watch | the big gate |
because they were getting bored**
Numerologist Night | a crystal skull | the great tower | to per-
ceive a glimpse of the overall

46. "It was Hack Blaxton with an award in Midnight Studios. Why? Because he wanted respect!"

"Even the extra didn't respect me! I asked him what he thought of my last movie, and he said it was too simplistic and made to appeal to a broader audience. But I told him that appealing to everybody was a lot harder than appealing to a niche audience. And he told me that it didn't appeal to everybody because it didn't appeal to him. And that's when I hit him with this award."

Logico eyed the murder weapon. "Is it yours?"

"Argh!" Hack shouted, as he lunged at Logico. (It was not his award.)

Thankfully, Logico was able to use his years of college chessboxing in order to avoid the assault.

**Hack Blaxton | an award | Midnight Studios | because they
wanted respect**
Midnight III | a DVD box set | the Magic Palace | to save cinema
It-Girl Abalone | a "prop" knife | the Hollywood sign | just be-
ing wild and famous in LA
Director Dusty | a cursed screenplay | the freeway | to get a
great shot

47. "It was Grandmaster Rose with a chess book in the rooftop lounge. Why? To prove his own superiority!"

"And I've done it! And I haven't just proven my own superiority—I've proven the superiority of logic itself. Because without logic, I never would have committed that crime. But with logic, I was able to do it effortlessly. And only another brilliant logician like yourself could catch me!"

Logico was really starting to question the title of his dissertation: "Why Logic Is Always Good." He was also starting to question some of his life decisions.

> Coach Raspberry | boxing gloves | the ring | to destroy the competition
> Pro Chessboxer Blaze | a mysterious package | the stands | to be the world champion
> Has-Been Gold | a folding chair | ringside | to be remembered forever
> **Grandmaster Rose | a chess book | the rooftop lounge | to prove their own superiority**

48. **"It was Ex-Chancellor Oak with a flag in the actual courtroom! Why? Because logic demanded it!"**

And Logico was struck by the thought that this person, who was so logical, would once again let logic drive him to murder. Maybe there was something to the iron-clad rigidity of logic that made it dangerous.

> Officer Copper | a bag of cash | the jury deliberation room | because they knew they'd get away with it
> Captain Slate | a gavel | the parking lot | as a trial run
> Judge Pine | the scales of justice | the judge's chambers | to prove their authority
> **Ex-Chancellor Oak | a flag | the actual courtroom | because logic demanded it**

49. **"It was Dr. Seashell, DDS, with an impossible triangle in the sonic oscillator. Why? To prove his theory!"**

"When you disproved my skepticism back in college, I went away and developed the perfect philosophy that explained all of the cosmos. And if it needed me to kill someone, I had to do it. Wouldn't you do whatever logic demanded?"

But Logico didn't know anymore. He wandered outside and looked up at the stars, and he looked at the constellation of the impossible triangle in the sky above him.

He felt himself pulled upward and outward, like he was rising off the ground.

And he saw, in the stars in the sky, a future that he had forgotten.

He saw everything that he was going to do, the mysteries he was going to solve, the clues that he was going to find. He saw the world as it was and as it could be, and he knew, as clearly as he had ever known anything, that Irratino must be innocent, that logic could guide you, but it should never control you, for while your feet may be planted on the ground, you eyes must be aimed up at the stars. And suddenly he realized the truth. Or, rather, the Truth.

And he knew what he needed to do.

> Mayor Honey | Ouija board | a crystal shop | to stay in power
> CEO Indigo | a crystal ball | the town square | to protect their secret plans
> **Dr. Seashell, DDS | an impossible triangle | the sonic oscillator | to prove their theory**
> Sir Rulean | a deck of marot cards | a UFO crash site | to show off

50. "It was Chancellor Tuscany with an ivory scepter in Old Main! Why? To take over the school!"

This led to gasps from the other people at the dinner, and many of them had objections, but the more Logico went over the evidence, the clearer it was.

"From the very beginning, I've known that her motive was to take over the school (see Case 10: Big Corpse on Campus). Once she was there, she wanted to maintain power (see Case 41: Murder Around the World). Obviously, she would do anything to take control. In the course of only four years, she moved from the job of assistant professor to the job of chancellor, and the only way that was possible was by the destruction of everyone who stood in her way."

Why would a secret society advertise that the school was going to die? If they were going to destroy the school, they would have done so in secret! However, someone wanting to eliminate a secret society, and a threat to her control, would have a great benefit in creating the appearance that a secret society was plotting against her. But how did I know she had made her own effigy? Because of the red tape used to affix the threat to it! That same red tape was in Chancellor Tuscany's office in Old Main! (See Case 41: Murder Around the World.)"

Did you know that Chancellor Tuscany was behind it all? If so, give yourself an extra five gold stars. And give yourself two gold stars if you noticed the red tape!

But while the murderer's identity was clear, Logico still didn't understand many of the details. But after the confrontation at the dinner, Inspector Irratino met him in the quad.

"You exonerated me again, Logico. I'd thank you, but I know you're just going to tell me that you only followed your deductions from first principles."

"This time, it wasn't just reason," Logico said. "This time, I wanted to do it."

"Why?"

"I don't know, really," Logico replied. "I just did."

"Then you're ready to learn the truth," Irratino said. He handed Logico a letter.

"What is this?" Logico said.

"The answer to all of your questions is inside."

And you can read it yourself in Appendix E.

Inspector Irratino | a ruby pin | the quad | to destroy the college

Chancellor Tuscany | an ivory scepter | Old Main | to take over the school

Coach Raspberry | the championship trophy | the chessboxing gym | to win, win, win

Dame Obsidian | *How I Murdered My Husband* | the arboretum | for publicity

COMMENCEMENT

Add up the number of stars you received while solving these mysteries to determine the degree with which you'll graduate Deduction College:

0	No Degree (and no refunds, either)
1–19	Certificate of Deduction with a Minor in Lucky Guessing
20–34	A Bachelor's Degree with No Frills, Bells, or Whistles
35–49	A Bachelor's with Distinction or Magna or Some Other Fancy Qualifier
50–59	A Very Impressive Master's Degree in Deductive Reasoning
60+	The "Genius" Degree in Overachievement

How did you do? If you graduated at all, that's worthy of congratulations! You can now call yourself a deductive detective, just like Logico! If you didn't graduate, that's okay, too.

It turns out a degree from a college where fifty murders were committed is not exactly the world's most prestigious accomplishment.